"Don't cry because it's over, smile because it happened."

~ Dr. Seuss

"Life is not measured by the number of breaths we take, but by the moments that take our breath away."

~ Anonymous

"I'm selfish, impatient and a little insecure. I make mistakes, I am out of control and at times hard to handle. But if you can't handle me at my worst, then you sure as hell don't deserve me at my best."

~ Marilyn Monroe

CHASING *Nikki*

BY LACEY WEATHERFORD

Moonstruck Media - **Arizona**

Dedication

For my mom.
Thanks for always encouraging my dreams. Words cannot
express how much I miss you.
I love you so much.
Peggy Jackson
1949 - 2007

For Mike.
I was glad to know your amazing spirit for that short while.
You left far too soon.
Michael Dunham
1970-1989

Acknowledgments

I often look around myself, and life, for inspiration for what I write, and this story was no different. I've been a big fan of football for many years, watching my brother, Glen, make 1st Team All State and winning the Arizona state playoff as well. After that I was hooked for life.

I was watching a playoff game when I first came up with the idea for this story. It sat in the back of my mind for about two years until I happened upon a game with a new quarterback whose name was Chase Walden. I fell instantly in love with the way he played football in his "all-out-no-holds-barred" kind of style. When I finally had the chance to meet him off the field, I discovered he was a great kid, full of this natural swagger that just rolled easily off him. I knew I had found my muse for my story. Thankfully, Chase was intrigued with the idea as well, and agreed to let me use his name and likeness to build my fictional character. He helped me out with some of the current teen lingo, music for my playlist, and allowed me to pick his brain a bit when I needed. So thank you, Chase, for the help and inspiration you gave. It meant so much.

Life has also blessed me with many more amazing people, and bits and pieces of how they've touched me are blended into this tale too, helping to make up the story that revolves around Chase. I thank them for the lessons and memories they've left me with, namely my mom, Peggy, and my dear friend, Mike. What a gift it was to know you both.

And, of course, a special thank you to my business partners of Moonstruck Media, Bels and Kam, who work so hard to make sure everything always turns out just right.

I love you all!

Part One

~Chapter One~

I took a deep drag from the joint before passing it to the girl next to me. She clasped it easily, lifting it between her plump lips. I watched her inhale deeply before I looked away, turning back to concentrate on the fire dancing in the dirt ring before me. My eyes wouldn't adjust though, and it kept swimming in and out of focus.

Man, I'm cross-faded already, I thought. Then again it would probably be more surprising if I weren't, considering how much I'd been partying lately. If I were being totally honest, my days were starting to run into one another. My life was definitely not what it had been before . . . everything . . ., but I didn't want to think about that.

I reached for the bottle of beer sitting on the ground and lifted it, taking a heavy swig. I didn't even notice the bitter taste anymore. I was feeling numb, and that's exactly the way I wanted it.

"Hey, Chase." The girl leaning against me nuzzled the underside of my jaw line, placing a little kiss there as she traced a finger down my chest. "Wanna get out of here and go someplace we can be alone?"

"Maybe later . . . um . . . ," I chuckled as I pushed her away slightly with my elbow.

"What's so funny?" She stuck her bottom lip out in a pout as she stared at me.

"The fact I can't remember your name," I replied bluntly.

"You're a jerk!" she said, shoving me and walking away.

I caught myself before I fell to the side. "Yes, I am!" I shouted at her retreating figure, and I tossed back another long swallow of beer. I did feel sort of sorry. I really should remember, seeing as we'd been dating for weeks now.

I glanced to where my friend, Connor, was making out with his girlfriend. It was funny, but I could remember his name fine. I gave another chuckle and leaned against the large rock behind me, closing my eyes. I must not be blitzed enough yet.

Someone shook me, and I woke with a start, not realizing I'd fallen asleep. For a moment, I was unsure where I was.

"Hey, buddy. Where are your keys?" Connor's voice broke into my hazy thoughts.

"Keys?" I questioned, confused.

"Yeah. You're too drunk to drive, and my mom is threatening to send my dad looking for me if I'm not home in the next thirty minutes."

"Not cool."

"Yep. Party's over, bro."

I grabbed my beer and slowly got to my feet while Connor hollered over his shoulder for the two girls to get in the truck.

He turned toward me, narrowing his eyes a bit before letting out a laugh. "Feeling a little unsteady there?"

"Maybe," I replied with a grin.

My friend offered me an arm, and I leaned heavily against him for support as we made our way to the vehicle. I briefly handed my drink to one of the girls in the truck so I could reach into my pocket to drag out the keys and hand them to Connor.

He helped me inside and closed the door before going around to the driver's side.

"Be careful with my truck. It's my baby," I joked as we started off down the bumpy road.

"It's in better hands than yours right now," Connor ribbed back.

"I thought I was your baby," the girl beside me said, squeezing my thigh with her fingers.

"Really? Hmm. Wonder where you got that idea," I replied as I lifted the bottle to my lips.

She sucked in a hurt breath and pulled her hand away, but I couldn't bring myself to care.

"You'll never make it home in time," the other girl whined as we left the desert road and turned onto the highway. "We're still at least twenty minutes away from town."

"Yeah? Watch me." Connor laughed, hitting the gas heavily. The engine revved loudly, and the truck shot off down the road, causing the scenery to flash by in the blur of headlights.

I closed my eyes, fighting the nausea the motion caused. All of a sudden I felt sick. Clenching my teeth, I gripped the door handle, trying to calm my stomach. I wrestled with the overwhelming sensation for several minutes before finally giving up.

"Dude, pull over."

"I can't," Connor replied. "My mom will kill me if I'm late."

"I'm gonna throw up, man. Pull over!"

Connor let out a stream of cuss words and hit the brakes so hard I felt like I was going to pitch right through the windshield.

"What the hell?" I yelled, as I braced myself against the dashboard and turned to look at him.

That's when I noticed the red and blue lights flashing behind the truck, and the sound of a short, clicking siren filled the air. I glanced down at the container of beer I had tucked between my legs and started laughing.

Yep, I thought, dragging a shaky hand through my short dark hair as the truck came to a complete stop. *Tonight is about to get fun.*

I opened my door and puked.

The door to the holding cell clanked open loudly against the wall, and I groaned as I held my head in between my hands. Were all jails this loud, or was I being specially punished? Wasn't it enough I'd spent most of the night vomiting into the corner toilet? At one point I was almost sure death would've been more beneficial.

"You reek," a soft voice said, and for the first time I felt a real momentary stab of regret as I looked up into my mom's face. I quickly moved my gaze back to her feet so I wouldn't have to see the disappointment in her eyes and noticed the boots of an officer walking toward me.

"Time to go home, son. Your mom has posted bail." He grabbed me by the elbow.

"I'm not your son." I yanked my arm from his grasp. "Back off."

"Look, Mr. Walker, we can do this the hard way or the easy way. It's up to you." He took hold of me once again.

I growled under my breath and turned aggressively toward the man, intent on showing him a thing or two, jail time be damned.

"Chase." My mom's voice had almost a pleading quality to it. "Please. Haven't we been through enough?"

I turned and saw tears brewing in her eyes. Guilt returned to prick at my conscience. I clenched my jaw so hard it felt like my teeth might break, but I backed down. A few minutes later I watched as my mom signed her name—Tori Lynn Walker—with a flourish, and I was allowed to leave the police station in her custody.

"Where's my truck?" I asked, scanning the parking lot.

"Where do you think it is? It's been impounded."

"Are we going to get it now?"

"No." She hit the clicker on her key chain to unlock the doors of her red Toyota.

"When, then?" I asked, trying to ignore the dull, pounding ache in my head.

She sighed heavily as she glanced at me over the roof of the car. "I'm going to sell it."

Suddenly the dull, pounding resembled a roar. "Excuse me?"

"No. Excuse me, but I can't take watching you drink your sorry butt into oblivion anymore. You aren't being responsible. Having a vehicle is a privilege—one you clearly don't deserve. If you'd been the one driving it last night, you'd be in a whole lot more legal trouble than you are right now. Connor is being charged with the DUI. You've been charged with underage drinking and possession of an open container. From the smell on you, I'd say you were lucky there isn't a marijuana charge against you too." She slid into the car and slammed the door.

I did the same, intent on arguing and instantly regretted the movement, my head throbbing.

"So now what?" I leaned back against the seat, suddenly feeling too tired to fight. "Am I grounded? For how long?"

"Oh, it's going to be much worse."

"What do you mean?" I didn't like the tone of her voice.

"Well, first we have your court date on Thursday.

Then after we find out what the judge has in store for you . . . we're moving."

"What?" I said incredulously. "You can't do that!"

"I have, and we will!" She threw the car into gear and pulled from the parking space.

"Where?"

"To live with Grandma and Grandpa."

"You aren't serious, are you? Please, say you're joking! Do you really want to make my life a complete living hell?"

My mom hit the brakes hard as she came to the stop sign, turning to stare at me. I could see the anger written plainly on her face, but when she spoke her voice was soft again.

"The only person responsible for making your life hell is you, Chase."

"Mom," I groaned. "Please don't."

"It's done. I'd already been talking to them about it. I made the plans final as soon as I found out you were arrested last night. Grandma and Grandpa are waiting for us."

"I can't do this. Don't take us there. It'll be worse than it is here. There's no possible way for me to fit in. It's like Hicksville! Even Dad hated it. Grandpa is totally insane and . . ." my voice trailed off when I saw the hard look in her eyes.

Neither of us spoke again for the rest of the ride home, but I was biting the inside of my mouth in an attempt to keep my comments from spewing out. I knew it would only hurt her more, and despite everything I'd done to add to her burdens, it had never been my intention. I wasn't trying to be bad or make things harder. I was only trying to forget it all.

The memories resurfaced for the millionth time, despite my desperate attempts to ignore them.

"Happy seventeenth birthday, Chase!" my dad

said, smiling as he handed me the keys to the gorgeous, white extended cab Dodge Ram pickup, with dark tinted windows sitting in the driveway.

"Are you for real?" I exclaimed as I took them and hurried toward the truck. "I can't believe you got it!"

My dad laughed. "Well, it was either that or listen to you go on about it every time we drove past the dealership together. I even got it in your favorite color. I still think the cherry red one was better, though."

"No way. White is always the best," I replied, and he chuckled again.

"White isn't a color. It's . . . white, like the absence of color."

"I don't care. It's my favorite." I grinned as I opened the driver's side door and hopped in, running my hands in awe over the steering wheel before leaning over to check out the stereo system.

"So, do you like it then?" Dad's voice broke into my thoughts.

"I love it!" I said, sliding from the vehicle.

He clapped me into a big bear hug, patting me hard. "You deserve it. You're a great kid!"

"Thanks, Dad."

"Don't forget I love you," he added quickly. "Now get to school, and hurry straight home after football practice tonight. Mom's going to need some help with your party."

"Yes, sir." I smiled, bending to pick up my backpack I had dropped on the concrete.

"Sorry I won't be there. I'll try to call you tonight from Denver."

"Okay, sounds good. Hope your meeting goes well." I climbed inside the truck and started it.

He stood in the driveway, waving at me as I drove away and headed to school.

Later, I came home from practice to find my mom

sobbing on the couch, nothing ready for my party.

"What's the matter?" I asked, dropping my gear and hurrying to her side.

"Your dad's secretary called. His plane crashed on the way to Denver."

"What?" My heart sank. "Is he okay?"

"No one onboard survived."

Her words seared into me, sinking like a branding iron, burning through every layer, and for a moment I forgot to breathe.

I took a deep gasp now, bringing myself back to reality as I realized I was holding my breath once again. My hands were clenched into fists, and I flexed them, forcing myself to relax as I turned to stare out the window.

That was the day my life had turned for the worse. Everything, it seemed, started falling apart in that moment. My dad's estate was settled, and most of the money went to pay off the debts of our family's high-priced lifestyle. We lost our ritzy Canyon Heights home and moved from Scottsdale to a cheaper neighborhood in Mesa, Arizona.

I had to change schools, which caused me to lose my spot as quarterback on the football team, and the friends I had seemed to disappear into the woodwork. No one cared I was an all-star athlete at my last school. I went from being popular, to simply the new face in a sea of four thousand others.

A few kids from the partying crowd befriended me early on, and I quickly joined in with them, eager to escape the thoughts banging around in my head. They invited me to hang out over the weekend, and when they passed the blunt to me, it suddenly seemed just the thing I needed. A little something I could get lost in to help take the edge off. All it took was one time, and I was hooked. I'd never really considered myself the drug and alcohol type, but that soon changed. I lived for the next party, knowing I'd be able to sink into the blissful numbness awaiting me there.

I tried to hide my new lifestyle from my mom in the beginning, and was fairly successful. Over time though, I started growing more careless as I sunk deeper into my new hobby, and she started growing suspicious. I knew she was catching on when she started grilling me about being late and who I was with.

I became the master of evasion, unwilling to give up the new world I'd created for myself. She started grounding me for breaking the rules, or she would take away my phone and truck. I quickly solved this problem by keeping a stash hidden in my room, breaking it out when she would leave for work, or I'd lock my door, turn up the music and climb through the window onto the roof to smoke.

My dealer was a hot girl from school, and I started dating her. Sometimes she would come party with me all day at the house. My mom never knew some of the worst things I'd ever done happened right in my own bedroom while she was punishing me. Thankfully, she'd never caught on.

I had a nice system going, and I thought things couldn't get any worse—until now. Now my mom was dragging me to live on a ranch in the middle of Podunk-freaking-nowhere with my psychotic grandpa who believed ranching was the be-all, end-all, to learning life's lessons.

Even before my dad died, I hated going to visit because all I ever did was work. I'd spent entire vacations feeding cows, straining milk, planting giant fields of corn, and mucking out stalls until I was sure the manure smell would never come off.

I quickly learned to create reasons not to go by joining all the sports teams at school. Games and practices didn't allow me to leave town much. During the summer I worked as a lifeguard for one of the local pools, and trips to grandpa's house became fewer and farther between. My dad volunteered to stay home with me, sending Mom away to see her parents by herself.

The car pulled into the driveway, and I hurriedly exited the vehicle. I rushed into the house ahead of my mom and locked myself in my room. I sank down on the bed, stretching out to bury my face into the pillow.

Her declaration shocked me. Looking back, I probably shouldn't have been surprised. Yes, I could admit I was on a massive downward spiral—failing classes, not playing sports—not caring about anything in general. I submersed myself in partying and trying to cover the hurt inside. Mom threatened on several occasions that I better straighten up my act, or I wouldn't like the consequences. I thought it was all talk though, and never did I think she would resort to moving again.

Silver Creek, Arizona. I couldn't believe it. I'd never survive there. There wasn't anything to do—unless kids really were into cow tipping these days. And the only weed a teenager could score was probably the ones growing on the sides of the road.

I slammed my fist into the headboard and felt my knuckles split open. I looked to see the blood running down my fingers before I flopped back to my pillow.

Let it bleed, I thought. *I don't even care.*

My phone buzzed in my pocket. I dug it out, seeing the battery was nearly dead since it hadn't been charged during the night.

U home? The screen showed a text from Conner.

Ya, U?

Ya. Dad yelled 4 an hour. Says I'm going 2 jail.

I felt sick to my stomach. Sorry, bro. I typed back. Guess we finally got caught.

Guess so. Mom's making me move 2 Silver Creek—with my grandpa.

Man! I think I'd prefer jail, Connor replied.

The phone buzzed once loudly as it died. I tossed it onto the nightstand and buried my face back into the pillow.

Everything was so messed up.

"The sentence is a five hundred dollar fine, and one hundred hours of community service, as well as a weekend rehab session on the destructive nature of alcohol and drug use." The judge's gavel struck down, and I tried to keep my expression neutral as I left the courtroom.

"You got off easy, if you ask me," Mom said once we stepped outside.

"Easy? You're kidding, right?" I complained. "What do I need rehab for? I'm not addicted to anything."

"You might not be, but you've been abusing substances, and addiction usually follows. I think it's a good call on the judge's part."

I kept my mouth shut. Arguing wasn't going to do anything but get me into more trouble.

"You're lucky. If you had been caught at school they could've suspended you and kicked you out of sports— not that it matters since you haven't played anything since football season anyway."

"So now what?" I asked, wanting to get off the subject.

"Now you're going to pay the fine from your checking account. Then we'll make an appointment with the court liaison so we can get your rehab and community service transferred to Silver Creek."

I groaned. "Please, Mom. Isn't there any way I can talk you out of this? I promise I'll be better. Just stay here."

"No, my mind is made up. I think the change in environment will be good for both of us. It'll be nice to feel like part of a family again."

Not Grandpa's family, I thought. The guy was a hardnose about everything. He expected things to be done a certain way, at a certain time, and you couldn't argue with him. I knew part of my grandpa's attitude came from being a corpsman in the Marines in his younger years. He'd learned to love rigid order, and he brought that into his everyday life when he left the service.

"It'll be like living in the middle of a military barracks," I grumbled, pausing at the door to the office my mom was ushering me into.

"Maybe it won't be as bad as you think," she replied, looking up at me. "We can both use a little structure in our lives right now."

"Speak for yourself," I replied under my breath, but she heard every word.

"Do you remember where we're at?" She arched an eyebrow. "I don't need any more attitude."

"Let's get this over with," I said with a sigh and walked quickly through the door, but she grabbed my arm, turning me back to face her.

"Chase, I only want what's best for you. Trust me." Her direct look was full of emotion, and it caused me to feel a moment of regret again. I couldn't hurt her any more than I already had. She didn't deserve it.

"I'm trying to, Mom. I really am."

~Chapter Two~

I drove my truck up the dirt lane—following the small U-Haul my mom was driving, towing her car behind it. We had to go slowly since the road was full of dips and bumps caused by heavy snow and rain during the winter. I was thankful it was April, and while it was still cool, we'd missed the worst of the weather. I was definitely going to miss the warm desert. I sighed again, for what must've been the thousandth time and cranked my music up louder.

At least I'd managed to convince her to let me keep my pickup. I reminded her the ranch was three miles off the main highway and three more miles to the school. Unless Grandpa was planning on loaning me his ancient tractor, she was going to have to take me to school every day, because I refused to walk three miles to catch the bus.

She finally relented.

We passed out of the heavy cedar growth into the flat area that marked the ranch. The fields were all empty dirt patches waiting to be replanted.

Silver Creek—the actual creek the town was named after—ran through the far edge of the property. Big cottonwood trees lined its banks, their new spring leaves rippling in the breeze. Directly ahead was the sprawling two story white ranch house, with its immaculately trimmed lawns and wide porches. The huge red barn, with lots of stalls and corrals, sat off to the right.

I guess people would call the view pretty, if they were into rural settings. I, personally, thought it would have been more appropriate if there were a giant sign in the yard with the word 'PRISON' scrawled across it in giant letters.

Grandma Johnson ran from the house with a big smile on her face as we pulled up. She wiped her hands on her apron and hurried to greet us. Mom jumped out to hug her, and I reluctantly went to do the same. Grandma was probably the one bright spot to this whole new change, but I wasn't in the mood for happy greetings.

"Chase!" She turned with a delighted look and held her arms open.

I walked into them and hugged her loosely, but she squeezed me tightly.

"Welcome home," she said. "I'm so thrilled you've come to live with us. We've hardly seen you it seems, and I can't believe how big you've gotten! How tall are you now?"

"Six foot two," I replied, stepping away.

"My, my, and all lean muscle from the looks of it. I bet the girls go nuts over you with your strong, chiseled jaw, dark hair and eyes. You've grown like a weed! Ah, so handsome." She clasped a hand over her heart.

At the mention of weed, I suddenly wished I had some. I could use a little escape right now. It was one thing to have cute babes hanging all over me, another entirely to have my grandma raving over how good-looking she thought I was. It was a little creepy.

My thoughts were interrupted by a new figure stepping from the house.

Grandpa Johnson was imposing. He was tall and fit, with short, salt and pepper colored hair. I could hear his boots hitting the porch as he crossed and made his way down the steps toward us.

"They're here, Warren!" my grandma called.

"I can see that, Caroline," he replied gruffly. He bent to hug my mom. "Welcome home, Tori, sweetheart."

"Thanks, Dad," she replied happily.

Grandpa moved away and turned to look at me. He scowled, and I lifted my chin, determined not to let him walk all over me. "Chase," he said in a low voice.

"Warden," I replied with a sarcastic nod, telling him I knew exactly what his intended role was in regard to me.

His jaw clenched, but to his credit, he didn't give into my goading, and there was an awkward silence before Grandma spoke to my mother.

"We've prepared the upstairs for you. Your dad and I rarely go up there anymore, so feel free to arrange your things however you would like. Anything of ours you don't want to use can be taken to the attic."

"No worries, Grandma," I said. "We hardly own anything these days. I think Mom sold almost all our stuff, didn't you?" I cast a glare at her as I walked over to open the U-Haul. "Two couches, beds, office stuff, and our clothes. Not much left."

I grabbed a box and headed toward the house.

"I'm sorry about him. He's a little angry," Mom apologized as I passed by.

"Don't worry. We'll teach him some manners," I heard Grandpa reply, and I shook my head in disgust and kept on walking.

I lounged on the bed in my new room, which was small but adequate, listening to rap music early that evening. Exhausted from moving everything in, I just wanted to go to sleep, but my mom appeared in the doorway.

"How you doing?" she asked after I pulled one of

the ear buds out so I could hear her.

"As well as can be expected." I shrugged. "Why?"

"Grandpa wants you to help him with the evening chores." She had the decency to look apologetic as she said it.

"Ugh," I answered with an eye-rolling sigh as I sat up. I grabbed my shoes next to the bed and began putting them on. "I guess it's time to let the warden work the evil out of me. Wait. Doesn't that make him an exorcist?"

She actually snickered at the comment, and I scowled. I took my hoodie off the back of the chair and headed out the door.

"Hey," she said, stopping me. "Take it easy on him, okay?"

I raised an eyebrow in disbelief. "Take it easy on *him*?"

"He opened his home to us because he loves us. He may show it in different ways, but that doesn't mean it's any less real. Besides, he's not the one you're really mad at, so don't take your anger out on him because he's an easy target."

I snorted as I walked down the hall. "I don't think anyone would ever call him an easy target."

I entered the giant barn and looked around for Grandpa. I didn't see him, but I saw the old brown mare I used to ride when I was younger eating in her stall.

"Hey, Mitzi," I said, calling her by name as I walked over to pet her. "Do you remember me?" She bumped her nose against my chest, and I knew she was searching for goodies in my jacket. "Sorry, girl. I didn't bring anything with me this time. It's nice to know the old man still treats you good though."

"The old man has some carrots for her in the bucket on the shelf behind you," my grandpa's voice broke in.

"Oh, thanks," I said, staring at him before turning

to get a couple. He came and stood beside me, while I fed her.

"She's a good ol' gal. I don't have much use for her anymore, but I can't seem to get rid of her."

There was an awkward pause, neither of us really knowing what to say to each other. Grandpa gave a sigh and went to sit on a bale of hay, gesturing for me to sit across from him.

Here it comes, I thought, but I kept my mouth closed and did as he asked.

"So, you've been in a bit of trouble lately," he started, and I could feel myself getting a little frustrated. "Now before you go snapping at me, why don't you hear what I have to say first?"

I didn't trust myself to speak, so I gave him a curt nod.

He continued. "I know you've been through a lot in the last few months since your dad died. I'm also aware of what it's like to lose someone who's close. It's okay to grieve, and everyone should. There are lots of stages to go through, and while I don't know where you are, if I were to guess I'd say you're angry and hurt. I think you're trying to numb your pain."

I couldn't say anything. He was hitting the truth unbearably close, and I wasn't ready for this discussion. I needed to get out of here. I stood and headed toward the door.

"Chase," he called. "I'm not trying to counsel you. I just wanted to give you the opportunity to get off this ranch and do something else."

This surprised me, stopping me dead in my tracks. "And what would that be?"

He walked up beside me. "I'm a volunteer coach at the high school. I want you to come join the guys on the football team for our spring weight training. I know you quit last season after your dad died, but you have a great talent, and I don't think you should waste it. The head coach has already agreed to check you out as quarterback, since ours will graduate this year. There would be a lot of practices and summer camp too. I'm not promising anything. It would require hard work and responsibility, but it would give you something to do besides be here all the time."

Anything would be better than that, and I used to love playing football. "What's the catch?" I asked, wondering why he was going so easy on me.

"No catch. I think it'll give you something new to focus on. Plus, we need someone to step up and try for this spot. This isn't like the big city. We have to make do with what we've got. That being said, we have a really talented line, and I think our defense can hold their own too. They're a hard-working bunch of boys."

I didn't know what to say. I hadn't been expecting him to offer me a way out.

"You can think about it for a few weeks. Weight training won't start until the first of May," he added when I hesitated.

"Okay," I replied with a nod. I glanced around uncomfortably. "Mom said you wanted me to help you with the chores."

"I have most of them done for tonight, but I'd like to give you a few regular ones. I thought you could help take care of the stalls in here, keep them mucked out and lined with fresh straw. There are six stalls, but only three horses. You can put them in the empty ones or out into the corral while you clean. It'll only take about twenty minutes to do each of them."

He reminded me where all the equipment was located and showed me where the new trap doors had been installed in the hayloft, making it easier to shovel the fresh straw into stalls.

"Does this sound okay to you?" he asked cordially.

"Sure. I can take care of it."

"Thanks for your help, Chase." He clapped me on the shoulder and headed toward the house.

"Grandpa," I called, and he turned to look. "I'll do it—play football, I mean."

He stared at me for a moment, and I thought I could see a slight smile playing near the corner of his mouth. "Good," he replied, and walked away.

~Chapter Three~

I'd successfully survived my first three classes at Silver Creek High School, home of the Fighting Timberwolves. I had yet to see anything too impressive, despite how much my mom raved about this place.

I walked into my fourth hour history class and saw Brett Dodson, who I'd met in my first hour, along with his super cute twin sister, Brittney. They were both really friendly, but Brittney's boyfriend, Matt, didn't seem to care for me much. Of course, that may have been due to the fact I kept checking his girl out during class. I didn't plan on hitting on her since she was taken, but I thoroughly enjoyed watching him squirm when she would flash shy smiles back at me. It was funny.

Brett, on the other hand, seemed as if he'd decided to take me under his wing. He'd pretty much filled me in on the football team and what he felt their chances were to take state next year—who was hot, and who was not—along with the best places to eat lunch. He waved me over to sit by him.

"Hey dude," I said, scooting into the available desk.

"Welcome to one of the most boring classes on the planet," Brett said.

"Great."

"Yeah, this hour is perfect for a pre-lunch nap. Of course, you might get an eraser thrown at you if you do. Mr. Ralston doesn't take too kindly to that."

I stopped paying attention to him when a gorgeous,

perky brunette entered the room. She was laughing about something with her friend, flashing a beautiful smile of straight teeth and plump lips.

Suddenly the day was looking up.

"Who's that?" I asked with a nod toward the door, and it was almost like she heard, turning to stare straight at me with her big brown eyes.

I knew it was rude, but I couldn't look away. My glance traveled from her face, to her loosely crimped, shoulder length hair, down over the tight, black shirt and blue jeans that showed off all her curves. This chick was smokin' hot!

"Don't waste your time, man," Brett said, as the girl turned away and headed to a desk at the front of the room. "She won't give you the time of day."

"Why not?" I asked, still staring.

"Her name is Nikki Wagner, and she's sworn off any guy who plays football, even though she's a cheerleader."

I gave him a puzzled look. "What does football have to do with anything?"

"She used to go out with Jeremy Winters. He's a senior, and the varsity quarterback. I guess he decided their relationship was ready to go to the next level, but she didn't. She caught him in his car with another girl. When she found out the guys on the team knew he was seeing the other chick behind her back, she branded us all losers."

I leaned into my seat and crossed my legs in front of me as I stared at her again. "So you're saying she's a good girl, then?"

"Yep."

"Just as well. She probably wouldn't like me at all." I made up my mind to forget about her.

The teacher entered the classroom as the bell sounded and headed to the front. "We have a new student. Mr. Walker, can you please come up here?"

I couldn't help the soft groan and eye roll that sent Brett into a chuckle. I got up and went, wondering why every teacher today had seen the need to introduce me in front of the entire class.

"Everyone, this is Chase Walker. He's new here, and you should all make him feel welcome."

I was starting to wonder if they made the teachers rehearse this speech as part of their job training.

"Chase, why don't you tell us something interesting about yourself?"

Nikki was staring at me intently, and all of my attention zeroed in on her. I didn't register the question until I heard Mr. Ralston call my name again.

"Chase?"

There were snickers throughout the room, and I looked around. "Something interesting? Well, let's see. I was arrested for underage drinking. My mom decided some good ole fashioned country living might be exactly what I needed, so she forced me to move here."

"Uh, okay," Mr. Ralston stuttered, caught off guard by my reply. "That wasn't exactly what I meant. I was thinking more along the lines of things you like to do, or activities you're interested in."

I turned, looked straight at Nikki and smiled. "I like to do girls, and I'm interested in football." I could hear the gasps of shock and laughter as I walked back to my seat, leaving the teacher gaping where he stood.

"Dude, you rock!" Brett said when I slid into my desk.

"He asked." I shrugged. "I was just being honest."

"Mr. Walker, please see me after class," Mr. Ralston spoke up with a disapproving look on his face.

"Yes, sir," I said seriously, with all the politeness in the world.

When class was over I saw Nikki stand up. I waited

until she was about to pass my desk and stood, blocking her path.

"You're a punk," she said, and I noted that I liked the sound of her voice.

"And you're a quick learner," I replied, winking as I cast my gaze down her form once again.

She tried to push past, but I grabbed her arm, pulling her against me. "Tell me you like punks," I whispered into her ear.

"Let go." I did as she asked, but she didn't move away, instead narrowing her eyes. "Do those lines really work for you, pretty boy?"

"The name is Chase, and you should remember it because I'm coming after you, baby."

Her face flushed pink, and I knew then I had a true chance. She wasn't unaffected by me, and I was going to wear her down. She swallowed thickly, staring before letting out a huff and walking away.

I chuckled after her. As of this moment, Operation Chasing Nikki had begun.

The detention on my first day of school pretty much secured my reputation. Most of the student body had pegged me as the coolest guy ever, and the faculty had arrived at the conclusion I was now troublemaker number one to watch out for. It was cool with me. I didn't mind making the new friends, or being surrounded by all the doe-eyed girls who wanted me to pay attention to them.

All the girls but one—unfortunately for me, she was the one I was determined to have.

I let her stew over my previous comments for a couple days, not paying any attention to her when she walked into class, though I found myself staring at her back a lot during the hour. My personal resolve to forget about her had gone right out the window.

Something about her drew me. I thought of her a lot the past few nights while I was tending to the horse stalls for grandpa.

I'd received a stern lecture from him about my comment in class and how important it was to respect women. I let him say his piece, to get it over with. I didn't disrespect women. I adored them, but I didn't think he would approve of my adoration either, so I held my tongue.

The bell rang, signaling the release of class, and I watched Nikki hurry from her seat and through the door without looking in my direction. I grabbed my books and hurried after, catching up to her in the hall.

She cast one glance from the corner of her eye at me and started walking faster. "Go away," she said.

"Go out with me."

"No."

"Go out with me. I like you."

"You don't even know me."

"Exactly! That's why you should go out with me. How am I going to get to know you otherwise?"

"Not going to happen." She stopped at her locker and began twirling her combination.

"I'll bring you flowers. What's your favorite?"

No answer.

"What time should I pick you up? Is seven okay?"

"I'm not going out with you."

"Why? What's wrong with me? I brush my teeth, use mouthwash, and I wear oodles of deodorant." I placed my hand on the locker next to hers and leaned in really close behind her. "My aftershave is really nice too. Can you smell it?"

She paused in the middle of sliding her books onto the shelf and turned to look at me. "It does smell good, but I'm still not going out with you."

"Ah ha! A compliment! I knew it was in there

somewhere." I smiled widely. "I guess I'll cut my losses for today and run with my compliment. But don't worry, Nikki," I whispered into her ear. "I'll ask you again tomorrow."

She gave an exasperated sigh, and I laughed as I walked away.

"You're a sucker for punishment, you know that right?" Brett said from where he was standing against the wall watching.

"Are you saying you doubt my skills?" I asked, stopping at my own locker to drop off my books.

"Yes," he said bluntly.

"Ouch. I'm wounded. Guess I'll have to prove it to you."

"Why do you have to get her? Practically every other girl in the school is throwing herself at you, much to the dismay of the rest of us guys, I might add."

"I don't want every other girl." I glanced down the hall catching Nikki staring at me with a perplexed look. "I want that one." I flashed a wink in her direction and she quickly turned to hurry off with her friend. "You should go for the BFF. We could double date."

Brett shook his head. "Well, you're nothing if not persistent."

"I'm serious. Her friend is cute too. She'll go out with me easier if you're dating her best friend."

"Tana and I are old news, buddy. Sorry. That was over in like sixth grade."

"Really? How long were you with her?" I asked.

"A while."

"Was she any good? As a girlfriend, I mean."

He looked at me like I was crazy. "Yeah, she was the best hand holder in the world."

I chuckled. "No kissing yet, huh?"

"Nope. I had to save something for seventh grade." He actually rolled his eyes.

"Why'd you break up?" I asked.

"I don't know. It was sixth grade."

"I was worried hanging with you might be hurting my chances with Nikki if her gal pal is mad at you."

"Thanks for your concern," he said, dropping his head.

"Kidding, dude. Kidding." I laughed, punching him in the arm. "Let's go get some lunch!"

"Sounds good. I told Wes and Chad we'd meet them at Pizza Palace."

"Okay. Hey, what are you doing tonight? Do you have a date or anything?"

"No. Why?"

"You should come over and play video games or something. It looks like I'm not going to have a date this week either."

He grinned. "You aren't ever gonna have a date unless you start barking up a different tree."

"We'll see about that," I replied.

~Chapter Four~

"What are you doing?" Brittney asked me in a whisper as she followed my gaze. I was surprised to see her without Matt attached to her hip. I'd come to discover the guy was seriously one jealous dude.

"Shhh. I'm spying," I replied, as I hid in the alcove by the water fountain, giving myself a clear view of Nikki's locker but staying enough out of the way she wouldn't see me. "You better leave before Matt sees you talking to me. I swear he looks like he wants to beat the crap out of me every time I look at you. He doesn't like that I hang around with you and your brother. I thought he was going to croak when I showed up at your house last night to pick up Brett. He thought I was there to see you." I grinned at the memory.

She shrugged. "He'll get over it. I told him you were totally into Nikki. He says you don't stand a chance with her."

"Listen, I know he's all chummy with her ex, so he feels loyal to him, but I never back down from something I want."

She laughed. "I kind of got that after Brett told me about the little adventure you took him on last night."

I chuckled. "Brett's a whiner."

"Yes, he is, but don't tell him I said so." She tossed her long, blonde hair over her shoulder and smiled. "Well, good luck with your spying. I've got to get to class."

"See you later," I replied, watching her walk away

for a moment. She sure was a pretty girl, and I liked her. I wondered how she had ever ended up with a guy like Matt Wilson. She seemed too good for the likes of him.

I sighed and turned my attention back to my current conquest. Nikki walked up to her locker and right away noticed the sticky note I left for her, pulling it off to read it.

"Roses are red. Violets are blue. What will it take to go out with you?"

Her sigh was visible as she crumpled the note up in her hand and opened her locker. She gasped, and I laughed when the roses and violets fell out, showering her with flowers. She had no idea I'd been memorizing her combination when I stood behind her yesterday.

Perfect. I ducked away before she could see me and hurried to my first class, hoping I scored with this gesture. She made it clear she thought I was a player, and well, I really was. I'd had girlfriends in the past, but no one I was really committed to. I tended to notice all the girls in the general vicinity, looking for the next one who might be ready to replace the last.

I actually kind of found it funny I was trying so hard to get Nikki. True, I loved a good challenge, thanks to my naturally competitive nature, but never had I put this kind of effort into getting a date.

The bell rang right as I slid into my seat beside Brett in our chemistry lab.

"So, how'd it go?" he asked.

"Caught her completely off guard."

"Did she like them?"

"I don't know. Didn't stick around long enough to find out."

"She better like them. Especially since I had to drive to three different garden centers with you last night trying to find those stupid violet plants."

"Quit being a crybaby." I grinned as he rolled his eyes. He seemed to be doing that a lot lately.

"What are you doing this weekend?" he asked.

"I start my mandated community service. It's part of my sentence from the judge. I had to go to a weekend class on substance abuse and pay a five hundred dollar fine before I moved up here. Now I have one hundred hours to complete."

"Hmmm. So I guess you don't want to go partying with some of the guys from the team then, huh?"

I slouched in my chair. "I'd give anything to go. I told my mom I wasn't addicted to anything, but I have to admit the cravings have been pretty bad lately. I swear there are times I feel downright jittery."

"Man, that must suck."

"Big time. But with my family watching me like a hawk, I don't think it would be a wise choice right now. Maybe some other time."

"Well, here's a little something in case you need it." He reached into his jacket and flashed a joint.

I automatically took it and discretely slipped it into my pocket, a natural reflex I'd done a thousand times. Ironically, the action caused me to have difficulty concentrating through the rest of class. All I could think about was lighting up and relaxing.

I hurried into the hall after the bell rang and almost collided with Nikki as she left her classroom.

"Hey." I smiled.

She glared, and suddenly I was worried.

"Did you enjoy the flowers?"

"I sure did. They fell all over the place, and I had to stop to clean them up. It made me late, and I got a detention for being tardy. Thank you so much, but please keep your gifts to yourself from now on."

She stormed off down the hall, leaving me gaping.

"Well, you really botched things up," Brett's voice

came from over my shoulder. "Isn't that strike three now? I think you're out."

I ignored him and strode away in the opposite direction.

"How'd the spying go, Rockstar?" Brittney's voice interrupted as she fell into step beside me.

"Not the way I'd hoped," I replied. "My little prank got Nikki in trouble." I stopped and glanced down the two hallways in front of me. "Where's the principal's office? I keep getting all turned around in this confusing school."

She pointed in the right direction. "Good luck. I can talk to her at cheer practice if you need to me to."

"Thanks for the offer. I'll let you know."

I headed down the long hall until I found the office marked, Justin Woodside, Principal. "Hey. Can I serve detention for someone else if I'm the reason they got one?" I asked the secretary when I burst inside.

"Um, let me check," she replied with a fluster and picked up the phone.

A few minutes later, I was seated before Mr. Woodside. I explained what happened with Nikki and how in my own haste to get to class, I neglected to realize my actions would make her tardy also. I asked if I could please serve her detention. He looked at me like I was a little crazy.

"How about I tell her teacher about this, and we'll call it a misunderstanding on everyone's part?"

"That sounds great." I stood to leave.

"Wait," he replied, and I halted. "In return, give me your word you'll try harder to keep your nose clean around here. We don't need any more trouble makers."

I nodded and left the office after he had written a note excusing my tardy to my next class.

As soon as the dismissal bell rang, I jumped to my feet and hurried to look for Nikki. I was surprised to find her waiting by my door.

"Hey," I said, wondering what she was doing there.

"Thank you."

"For what?" I asked nonchalantly.

"For taking care of the detention. Mr. Woodside called me into his office and told me what you did." She shuffled her feet nervously.

"I didn't mean to get you in trouble. The flowers were supposed to be a friendly gesture."

"They were." She pulled her hand from under her book, and I saw she was holding one of the roses. She sniffed it and extended it toward me. "This one is for you."

"This could count as a gift, you know? People will start to think you like me," I teased.

She shrugged. "Oh well."

"Will you go out with me?" I asked again.

She smiled. "No. You and I wouldn't be any good together."

"I happen to disagree. I think we could make fireworks happen." I lifted the rose and tucked it into the hair behind her ear.

"That's why I can't do it, Chase. I'm sorry, but I played with fireworks before and got burned. I promised myself I would never date a guy like that again."

I stood staring as she walked away, not knowing what to say or think. I wasn't used to rejection, and I was surprised by how badly it hurt. I was also surprised by how much I felt the need to find her ex and rearrange his face.

The rest of the day passed in a blur, and for once I couldn't wait to get home. I was glad it was Friday, and I wouldn't have to look at Nikki all weekend. Maybe I could finally forget about her like she obviously wanted.

There was one thing I needed to do first. I found

Brett in the parking lot.

"Hey, man. What's up?" he asked when he saw me striding to where he was talking to Chad and Wes.

"You sure you can't come party with us, dude?" Wes asked, bumping fists with me.

"Not this time, but soon hopefully," I promised. "That's why I'm here though. Can any of you spot me some blunt right now? I can pay you for it." I pulled a twenty from my wallet.

"No worries. I can take care of you, bro," Chad said, and he reached into his backpack and removed a baggie. "There's more where that came from too."

Sweet. I'd found a supplier. "Awesome," I replied. "I appreciate it. Catch you guys later."

I walked away toward my truck and was certain of only one thing. I was getting high tonight.

Things worked perfectly. Grandpa was out of town acquiring some new equipment for the ranch, and he needed me to do all of the chores for him. I fed the animals as quickly as I could, and then went back to the house to do my homework.

Grandma called me down for supper, and I ate with her and my mom. If there was one thing I couldn't begrudge about living on the ranch, it was Grandma's cooking. I quickly dug into the fresh steak with the heaping side of mashed potatoes, gravy, and corn on the cob.

"So how was your first week of school?" my mom asked.

"It was okay," I replied in between bites.

"Just okay? You didn't make a lot of new friends?"

"Yeah. I did."

"Well, that's good isn't it?"

I shrugged. "I guess so."

"Hmm. You don't seem very excited about it. How

about the girls? Find anyone you might want to date?"

I put my fork down. "Mom, do we have to talk about this right now? The school is fine. I've made friends with some of the guys on the team. There are lots of cute girls, but I don't know if I'll be dating any of them soon."

"You should have some of the guys over sometime," Grandma interjected.

"I'd like that. I know at least one who would like to come play video games."

She covered my hand with hers. "This is your home too now. You can invite anyone you'd like to have here. I want you to be comfortable."

"Thanks, Grandma." I smiled. "How's your new job?" I asked my mom, trying to turn the focus off myself.

"It's a job. I don't know how much money I'll make in real estate here, and I guess this agency covers quite a broad area. So there may be times I'm gone for a few hours to show houses to potential clients."

"Well, I'm sure you'll be great at it."

"Thanks, Chase." She gave me a hug as she passed on the way to the sink, taking my plate with her.

"Grandma and I were thinking of going to a late movie since Grandpa is gone. Would you like to come with us?"

I shook my head. "No. I still need to muck out the horse stalls. I promised Grandpa I'd get a thorough cleaning done on them this weekend. I've got to go to Cooley tomorrow for my service hours anyway."

"Would you like us to stay here with you? We can go another time."

"No. Have some fun. You deserve it. I'll try to come next time."

"Okay, if you're sure."

"I'm sure." I felt a little guilty knowing what I had

planned, but I wasn't about to change my mind.

I made my way to the barn and finished up my work. When I had the last of the fresh straw in the stalls, I let the horses back in. I briefly spoke to old Mitzi and fed her a carrot before I climbed into the hayloft, pushing the top exterior door wide open. I leaned against the frame, and slid down to the floor.

The stars shone brilliantly against the clear night sky, and I lit up, drawing the smoke heavily into my lungs, closing my eyes as I sighed in relief.

Man, I'd forgotten how good this really was. I smoked one whole joint and immediately lit up another. The night was quiet—everything was so still. I didn't want to think about anything, willing all the voices in my head to be silent. There would be no death, moving, arrest, girls—only me, sitting in the night.

While that was nice in theory, it wasn't long before flashes of my dad popped into my head. I pushed them roughly aside, and they were immediately replaced with thoughts of Nikki.

I sighed. I need to let her go and find another girl. Any girl would do. She needed to be someone I could pass the time with. Maybe do a little partying, then some making out and who knows what else. I wasn't going to keep investing myself in trying to pursue a relationship that was going nowhere.

I snorted at my choice of words. Who was I kidding? There was no relationship. Sure Nikki was gorgeous, but we were complete opposites. She wasn't even my type. She was a good girl, and I was branded a bad boy. A punk, as she'd called me, and the problem was everyone else thought the same thing. No one had ever taken the opportunity to really get to know me before they passed judgment.

Maybe I didn't help my reputation at all, taking advantage of the times I could prove exactly how punk-like I could be, but what was the point of trying to be something else when everyone already had a preconceived notion of what you were?

They all thought they knew me, pegged me from the first glance. No one had any clue who I was on the inside. They didn't see the athlete who was determined to win, no matter the cost. They didn't see the raised bar I'd set for myself physically to be the best I could be. No one cared how hard I used to work on getting top grades before my dad died. He wanted me to get into a good college, and I wanted to do anything I could to make him happy. I wanted to get a football scholarship, but I was determined to have a high grade point average too when scouts looked at me.

I had an excellent employee record during my summer job as a lifeguard, receiving commendations for service from my boss. My job was always standing with him. He'd told me he would hire me anytime I could work because I was so reliable.

I had always been warm and friendly before. I was nice and polite to the people I met and formed, what I thought to be, lasting relationships with those around me. I was popular, well liked, and admired by many.

It never ceased to amaze me how everyone simply faded away into the background, melting slowly out of my life after my dad was killed. They couldn't understand how devastated I was by his death—how it felt like everything in my world had turned completely upside down.

He died on my birthday. On my birthday! I didn't ever want to have another one again. Every day I walked outside to get in my truck, and for one second I was standing on the carport hugging him before rushing off to school to show my friends my new gift. I didn't know it would be the last time I ever saw him as he stood in the driveway waving after me with a big smile on his face. I should have thrown a fit, begged him to skip work and stay home for my party. If I had he would be here, and we'd all still be living our real life, not this fake one which had risen up to take its place.

I never told him goodbye, and now I'd never have the chance again. The grief eating me up from the inside was unreal, unbearable. It became all-consuming, until it was the only thing I could think about. I couldn't concentrate on anything but the scenes of my dad flashing through my mind—how I'd taken everything for granted, assuming he would be there forever. It overwhelmed me until I couldn't take it anymore, and I was desperate to find a way to relieve the pain.

I jumped on the chance when it was offered, drowning my sorrows in alcohol and drugs. It didn't matter if it was wrong, I needed a way to escape, to be oblivious—a way to not feel like I needed to vomit every second of my waking life. I lived to get as drunk or high as I could . . . anything to move past that state of consciousness.

My problem now was no one was willing to look deep enough to see the real me lying dormant beneath the surface. Everyone thought I was a troublemaker, the bad boy, the punk.

I wasn't. I was just broken.

~Chapter Five~

"Can I help you?" asked the elderly woman behind the desk at Mountain Medical Center.

"Yeah, I'm Chase Walker. I'm here to volunteer for community service hours. The lady I talked to on the phone told me to check in here, and you would tell me where to go."

"Alright, let's see if we have you on the list," she replied, reaching for a clipboard and running a gnarled finger down the paper. "Yes, here you are. It says you're scheduled to assist in conference room B with the substance abuse group today. Go straight down this hall behind you, and make a turn at the second hallway to your right. The conference room will be there on your left."

"Thanks," I said, turning to follow her directions. *Substance abuse. That's just great,* I thought, wondering if the fates were starting to conspire against me too after last night.

I'd changed my clothes and thrown them in the washer after I left the barn, then scoured the house for some drops to help my bloodshot eyes. After I took a shower, I went to chill on my bed, planning to listen to my iPod while I waited for my mom and grandma to get home. Apparently, my body had other plans, since I fell asleep and slept clear through the night.

When I woke, I found someone had covered me with a blanket, and there was a box of candy from the theater placed on the nightstand. That was when I noticed the clock and realized I was running way behind. I jumped out of bed and hurriedly got ready to drive to Cooley.

I located the conference room easily enough, pausing at the door before I walked in. The room was empty except for a large circle of chairs in the center, but I could hear the murmur of voices coming through a door toward the back.

A tall, professionally dressed woman with graying hair pulled up into a bun appeared and looked at me quizzically. "Are you here for the group?" she asked.

"No. I'm supposed to help here today for community service," I replied.

"Ah, you're Chase." She smiled and stepped forward with an outstretched hand. "I'm Maggie Stafford. I'm the group therapist."

"Nice to meet you," I said politely.

"We're starting a new group this morning, and there's a massive amount of paperwork we pass out. You'll be helping my assistant organize packets and staple them together. There's a lot to do since we have exercises and journaling our participants are encouraged to do in their recovery therapy."

She motioned for me to follow her into the next room. "Because our group is large, our meetings will last about two hours. So if you work the entire time, I'll sign off on those for you."

"Sounds good," I replied, and she pointed me toward two long tables stretched out side by side. They were covered in massive stacks of paper.

I could hear other people entering the room we'd just left, and Maggie leaned forward to glance through the doorway. "I need to get out there. You can start by gathering the first five papers and stapling them together. My assistant will be back shortly to help you."

"Okay." I set my service paper down on a chair and

got to work.

It wasn't too long before I heard the hallway door open behind me.

"Here's the fresh coffee, Maggie. Sorry it took so long."

I stiffened and turned toward the voice.

"What are you doing here?" Nikki spoke, her eyes wide in surprise.

"I could ask you the same thing," I replied, folding my arms and leaning against the table as I gave her the once over. Yep, her effect on me was unchanged. Damn.

"I work here. I'm Maggie's assistant. Why are you here?" she asked again.

"You want to set the pot down? I don't want you to burn yourself," I replied, ignoring her question.

She seemed flustered for a moment, staring between the coffee and me before she carried it out to where the group was meeting.

I started stapling papers again, wondering why I was letting this stupid grin sit on my face. I reminded myself I'd decided to move on and forget about Nikki, but it didn't seem to help me any. Community service was suddenly looking a lot more fun.

She came back into the room and closed the door. "Did you follow me to work?"

I snorted, glancing at her out of the corner of my eye. "I'm not *that* desperate."

"Well?"

"Well what?"

"What are you doing here?" she asked, and I swore I saw her stomp her foot.

"I thought it was obvious. I'm stapling papers." I gestured to the rising pile before me.

She made an irritated sound, and I couldn't help but laugh.

"Did you just growl at me?" I raised an eyebrow as I

stared at her.

"Quit evading the question, and answer me." She was glaring now.

"I'm here to do court-mandated community service hours. It was part of my sentence after my arrest. I didn't know you worked here. This is one of those awe inspiring cosmic coincidences."

"Oh," she said, suddenly looking down at the floor. "I forgot you said you'd been arrested."

"You did?" I was surprised. Maybe there was hope for her after all. I was pretty sure everyone else imagined me wearing stripes everywhere I went. "People ask me about it so much I thought perhaps I had it stamped on my forehead."

"If you do, it's your own fault." She moved over—close enough I could smell her softly-scented perfume—and started gathering a packet of papers.

"How do you figure?"

"You don't let anyone forget it. You're always talking to others about it."

"I wouldn't say always. Besides, I'm just being honest. Don't want people to think I'm trying to hide who I really am."

"Is that who you are, Chase? A convicted underage drinker?"

"You tell me. You're the one who won't go out with me because of my reputation." I was beginning to feel a little angry. "Wait. I don't even think it's *my* reputation stopping you. It's your ex-boyfriend's, isn't it? What was his name again . . . Jeremy Winters?"

"I don't want to talk about him," she replied shortly.

"Fine. When you're ready to reveal everything about Mr. Winters, and why I must pay for his mistakes, then I'll tell you who I really am."

The only noises in the room were from both of us furiously grabbing papers and slamming them with the stapler. I was fuming, but I couldn't exactly place my finger on why. I just knew this whole situation irritated me.

I'd seen Jeremy and his entourage floating around at the school. He was a pompous jerk as far as I was concerned, but I played it cool around him because I was easily fitting into his crowd, hanging with the football friends we had in common. He'd be graduating in a few weeks, and I'd be taking his place on the team if I had anything to say about it. I'd prove then how much better I was than him.

I heard Nikki make a strange sound, and I looked up to see thin, wet trails streaming down her face.

Oh no. Not tears, I thought. *I don't know what to do with this.*

I stopped what I was doing and slipped my hand around her upper arm, directing her to the soft couch in the room. She sat, and I went to the cooler and got her a glass of water, snagging a box of tissues off the desk on my way past.

I handed her the items, and she took them without speaking.

"Spill it," I said, flopping onto the couch next to her.

"Wh . . . What?" she stuttered, looking confused.

"Tell me what's wrong."

"It's nothing."

"It's not nothing, or you wouldn't be crying. You can talk to me about it."

"I can't."

"Listen, Nikki, there isn't anything you can say to me that'll make me think any less of you. I've been through it all—heck, I've done it all. I'm not the person who's going to pass judgment on you. If you want to tell me to go to hell, then do it. I can take it. It won't be the worst thing someone has said to me." I paused. "I'm sorry if I offended you, by the way."

"I'm not mad at you." She pulled a tissue from the box and wiped her eyes, smearing her mascara.

"Here, let me help." I sat up and took a new tissue, dabbing at her face as I attempted to fix her makeup. The more I tried, the worse I seemed to make it, but it didn't matter when I realized she was watching me with a look of wonder. I froze, looking back into her big brown eyes, unable to move. Wow... she was so beautiful. I wished I could lean over and kiss her, but she was too vulnerable right now.

My thumbs replaced the tissue, wiping away new tears that leaked from her eyes. "What's wrong?" I encouraged her to talk again, loving the feel of her silky skin beneath my fingers.

She stared for several moments, struggling with whatever was bothering her. "He attacked me. I've never told anyone about it."

Ice ran through my veins at her words, and I leaned back. "He what?"

"I caught him with a girl in his car. We had a big fight, and he tried to tell me she was just a fling—that he had needs. I told him to get lost, and I broke up with him. He followed me home and burst into the house. He threw me on the couch and he... he... he would've succeeded if he hadn't heard the bus pull up to drop off my little brother and sister. He threatened me—said if I ever told he would come back and make sure to finish what he started. Then he ran out."

"Where were your parents?" I asked, floored by what she'd revealed.

"My mom works. My dad died from cancer a few years ago."

I silently kicked myself for adding to the burdens of this girl and the heartache she had been going through in her life.

"Nikki, I'm so sorry. You need to tell someone. This

guy needs to pay for what he did to you. It's illegal."

"I won't go through the humiliation of dealing with him again. I don't know why I told you. You were being so nice, and all of a sudden I couldn't hold it in anymore."

I pulled her into my arms gently, hugging her. "I'm glad you told me. I promise I won't let him ever hurt you."

She gave a half chuckle against my shoulder. "I wasn't asking you to be my white knight or anything. I just needed to tell someone. Have you ever had something you wished you could talk to someone about, but it's buried so deep you're almost afraid to give it a voice?"

I stared her in the face and nodded. "Every day, as a matter of fact. I understand completely. I really do."

"You don't have to share anything personal with me, because I did." She stood and walked over to the table. "I guess we should get these packets made."

I watched her as she started working again, quickly moving about her task. I didn't want her to feel even more awkward around me now. That's exactly what would happen if I didn't tell her something about me too.

"My dad was killed in a plane crash last year," I said as I joined her.

She glanced at me briefly and continued to work without speaking. I did the same, letting the silence hang in the air between us.

"Is that when you started acting out?" she asked after a few moments.

I laughed wryly. "If that's what you want to call it. I didn't do it on purpose. I only wanted to stop feeling what I was feeling."

"How bad was it?"

"Bad. I was willing to do, or try, anything to escape

it—sleeping, drinking, partying . . . girls."

"Drugs?" she asked point blank.

I sighed. "Yes, those too."

"What kinds?"

"Mostly smoking marijuana, but there were a few pills here and there. I never used those enough to become addicted though."

She turned to face me. "When was the last time you used?"

I swallowed hard, gritting my teeth. I didn't want to answer her. I wasn't sure how I'd started pouring my guts out to her, but I was pretty sure I needed to stop. I wasn't ready for this dam to break.

I continued my work, not answering. To her credit, she didn't try to press, but I still felt like a jerk after what she'd revealed to me.

"Last night," I finally replied. I felt a little sick. I could go to jail if she told anyone.

She was quiet for a couple of minutes before she spoke. "You would probably get more benefit from being in there with the group than being stuck here with me."

I chuckled sarcastically. "You're kidding, right? Nikki, you just got more out of me than I've been able to share with anyone in months. There's no way I'm gonna go and blab about myself to a bunch of strangers. That's not my style."

"You might be surprised how much Maggie could help."

"It isn't going to happen, so drop it," I snapped.

"I'm sorry. I didn't mean to sound pushy," she said softly.

I exhaled loudly and leaned on the table, focusing on the stacks. "You aren't pushy. I'm touchy about everything." I didn't know how to explain things.

"Well, I'm here. If you ever need anything, all you

have to do is ask."

I shoved away from the table and moved toward her. She took a couple of steps backward before standing firm.

"I did ask. I asked you to go out with me, and you said no. I understand why now, and you're right. He's a jerk, and I'm a player like he is, but I've never, ever forced myself on a girl, and I'm not about to start now. I can't promise you I won't do anything dumb, but I'll promise to be honest with you if you'll do the same with me."

She heard me loud and clear, I knew she did, so I continued on. "So here is what I need to know, Nikki. Do you *want* to go out with me? Or are you saying no because you're afraid?"

She looked like a cornered rabbit, and I felt horrible, but I wanted to know, once and for all.

"Why do you want to go out with me so badly? It doesn't make any sense. I'm not the type of girl you're used to being with." She swallowed nervously.

"I want to date you because you're the first person I've really noticed since my dad died. For the first time in a long time I want to do something besides get completely hammered. Is that so bad? It's a date. One date. If you like it, we'll have more. If you don't, we won't. I just want you to give me a chance before you decide I'm not worth it."

She walked away from me to the desk, running her fingers across the smooth surface. "Will you let me pick the time and place?" she asked.

I grinned widely. "Girl, you can do whatever you want as long as you say yes."

"Then yes. I'll go out with you." She smiled.

"Finally," I said, looking toward the ceiling and mouthing a thank you. I glanced back at her, and we both started laughing.

~Chapter Six~

I was still blissfully asleep at eight o'clock the next morning when my phone started buzzing. I reached to silence it, but when I saw the number I answered right away.

"Hello?" I tried to make my voice sound normal despite not having used it today.

"Are you awake?" Nikki asked.

"Of course," I replied.

"You said you would never lie to me remember?" She giggled.

"If I weren't awake, how could I be talking to you?"

"I woke you up, didn't I?"

"Yep, and I'm thinking you should do it every morning from now on." I couldn't stop grinning like a goof. "What's up?"

"I'm calling in our date. You said I could plan the time and place. The time is in one hour, and I will text you the address. Can you make it?"

"I'll be there." I hopped out of bed and hurried to my closet to pull out some clothes. "What are we doing?"

"Can't tell you. It'll ruin the surprise." She sounded excited.

"Okay. See you in a bit." I hung up and grabbed a couple other items and headed for the shower, passing my mom in the hall.

"Where are you headed so early?" she asked.

"I have a date," I replied with a wink.

"A date?" She smiled widely. "This early? On a Sunday? Must be a special girl."

"I'm thinking maybe so. Is it okay with you? I didn't ask. It was kind of spur of the moment."

"Who is she?"

"Her name is Nikki Wagner. She's a sweet girl. I guess she's one of the cheerleaders."

"Oh. A cheerleader," she replied in a voice that made it sound like I'd hit the jackpot or something. "Is she pretty?"

"Very. I'm in a bit of a hurry, Mom," I added, knowing the clock was ticking and not wanting to be late.

"Go on, kiddo. Have some fun for a change." She was humming to herself as she walked away.

Thirty-five minutes later I was running out of the house as I scarfed down a piece of toast with some jelly for breakfast. I cursed the dirt road for the bad condition it was in, causing me to drive slower.

When I got to town, I rushed into the supermarket, over to the flower section. They didn't have a whole lot to choose from, but there was a slender vase with three decent looking roses in it. There wasn't time to hit up the florist, and I wasn't sure if they were even open today. But I'd told Nikki I would bring her flowers when I first asked her out, and I intended to keep my word.

I was very antsy as I waited for the checkout line to move, knowing I was cutting it severely close. Thankfully, I sort of knew where I was going from the address Nikki had sent, and it wasn't far.

"Well, well. What have we here?"

I turned around to find Brett and Brittney grinning in the line behind me. They each held a box of doughnuts.

"I think someone has scored a date," Brittney said, winking. "Am I right?"

"I don't kiss and tell." I smiled.

"Ooh, and he's already talking about kissing. I think our little Rockstar thinks he's gonna get lucky today. What do you think, Bro?"

"Did she finally say yes?" Brett asked.

"Called me this morning and told me where to meet her." I glanced at my cell phone again. "And I'm going to be late if this line doesn't get going any faster. What are you two up to?" I said, trying to redirect the conversation.

"Out collecting the breakfast of champions." Brett gestured to the doughnuts.

"It's kind of a Sunday ritual with our family. Our parents started it before we were born," Brittney added.

"That's cool," I replied, happy to see it was my turn to check out. I did so quickly, grabbing the flowers and tossing a goodbye over my shoulder to the other two as I headed for the door.

"Have fun!" Brittney called after me.

"Absolutely."

I arrived at the location with one minute to spare. However, I was a little confused since I found myself sitting in the parking lot of a nursing home.

I checked her text again.

1225 E. Hillside Ave.

No, I was in the right place—she must've given me the wrong address.

I sent a message to Nikki. Umm . . . sitting in the parking lot of a rest home. Think U gave me the wrong address.

My phone buzzed. No. UR in the right place. Meet me in room 120.

This was an awfully strange place for a first date.

What the heck was she doing?

I stared at the text for a moment longer before I shook my head, wondering what I was getting into. I grabbed the vase of flowers and went inside.

"Can I help you?" a young man wearing a pair of scrubs asked when I walked into the large lobby.

"I'm meeting someone in room one twenty."

"Down the hall to your left." He pointed.

"Thanks." I went in the direction he'd indicated, passing several open doors along the way. There were a lot of people living here. I found the room number with the name Mildred Wagner etched into a little bronze plate underneath.

"Hello?" I called, knocking on the slightly ajar door.

"Come in, Chase," Nikki's voice replied.

I entered and found her curled up in a chair next to a bed that held a tiny, frail looking, elderly woman.

"Oh! You brought flowers!" Nikki exclaimed, getting up to come over.

"I told you I would." I smiled a little uncomfortably, still not sure why she was having me meet her here.

She took the vase. "Look, Grandma. Chase brought you flowers! Wasn't that sweet?"

I sighed and smiled, determined to play along with whatever she had going on.

"Chase, this is my Grandma Wagner. She's my dad's mom. He used to come and visit her every Sunday before he died. I've tried to keep up the tradition since he passed on. Grandma had a bad stroke several years ago and lost some of her motor and speech skills, so she's unable to take care of herself."

"Nice to meet you, Mrs. Wagner," I said, nodding toward the lady.

She gave me a half smile and slightly raised her trembling arm.

"She wants to shake your hand," Nikki said, placing the flowers on the bedside stand and sitting back down.

I walked over and took Mrs. Wagner's small hand in mine, giving it a slight squeeze. I was surprised by the strength with which she responded and continued her grasp, not letting go.

Nikki laughed. "I think someone has a crush. I told you he was very handsome, didn't I, Grandma?"

Mrs. Wagner visibly blushed at this remark, and I chuckled.

"I don't know what lies she's been telling you about me." I cast a glance in Nikki's direction. "But they're probably all true."

Nikki smiled wider. "Let go of him now, Grandma, so he can come sit by me."

Her grandma obliged, and I made my way around to the other side of the bed, pulling up a chair next to her.

"Every time I come here I make sure my grandma gets to eat her favorite pudding, which is butterscotch, by the way. She can't feed herself very well, so I like to help her enjoy her treat. Do you mind waiting while I do that first? Then we can go on the rest of our date."

"Sure. Do whatever you need to. I'm at your mercy for the entire day."

"I like the sound of that," Nikki said with a grin.

An orderly entered the room carrying what I assumed was pudding in a small parfait glass with a spoon.

"Here's your dish, Mrs. Wagner. Straight from the kitchen, just the way you like it." The young man smiled and served the dish toward her with a flourish, as if he were the best waiter in a fancy restaurant.

Mrs. Wagner gave her same half smile back to him.

Nikki took the dessert, sat on the edge of the bed, and began carefully feeding her grandma. She had to pause every now and then and wipe the woman's face with a napkin, but eventually she managed to patiently serve her every bite.

"Did you enjoy that?" Nikki asked her, and she

nodded. "Good. Would you like me to read to you a little before I go?"

Mrs. Wagner shook her head and pointed at me.

"You want Chase to read to you?" She giggled.

Her grandma denied her again and smiled wider, loosely gesturing toward the door.

"Oh. You want me to leave with him, don't you?"

Her grandma nodded and dropped her hand back into her lap.

"Well, I guess we've been kicked out, Chase. Let's go." Nikki picked up her bag off the nightstand before bending to kiss her grandma on the cheek. "Love you. I'll tell you all about it later, okay?"

"It was nice to meet you," I said again, patting the woman's hand, and she turned hers so she could clasp mine once more. She released me quickly this time, and I smiled before I followed Nikki through the door.

"She likes you," Nikki said with a grin.

"I think I might like her too. Of course, I don't really know her, but she seems as though she's a nice enough lady."

"She's wonderful. She also happens to be an incurable romantic. That's why she was so eager to rush us out of there."

"Really? Does that mean I should be expecting romance on this date you've planned?" I teased.

"You haven't qualified for that kind of attention yet, but you're getting closer," she replied.

"I haven't qualified? What is this, some sort of test or something?"

"Yep, and you're passing so far, so just chill and roll with it." She elbowed me in the ribs.

"It's a good thing I like you."

"Why's that?" she asked sincerely.

"Because I've never worked this hard to get a date before," I answered honestly.

She sidled up close and placed her hand on my chest. "Well, you know what they say. The best things come to those who wait." She bit her bottom lip and traced down with her finger.

My heart rate notched up a bit at her slight touch. "Is that what they say?"

"It is." She nodded.

"Well, then I guess I'll have to keep waiting."

She laughed, moving away, and I was sorry to see her go.

"So, where are we going now?" I asked.

"To the theater."

"Cool. What are we watching?" I could do a movie easily enough.

"Today is the Silver Screen Sunday Classic. We're going to watch *Gone with the Wind*. It's four hours of complete heaven."

I actually had to clench my teeth to keep the groan from escaping my mouth. "Sounds awesome," I said tightly, and she giggled even harder.

"There you go, breaking that whole lying promise again."

"I'm not lying—you and me, practically alone in a dark theater? That's right up my alley, I'd say."

She halted in the middle of the hallway. "Oh. I didn't think about that."

"I bet you didn't." I grinned, brushing past her. "But this was your idea so you can't back out now."

We stepped outside into the bright sunshine.

"Where's your car?" I asked, looking around for the red convertible VW bug she drove.

"I don't have it. My mom dropped me off today so I could ride with you later."

"Good thinking." I walked over to the passenger side of my truck and opened the door.

"Thanks," she replied softly, suddenly seeming kind

of shy.

"You're welcome," I answered, closing it once she was settled in.

She didn't speak while I drove, but it didn't feel uncomfortable, so I didn't try to break the silence. We soon had our tickets and were seated in the middle of the empty theater.

"Wow. I was kidding when I said it would be mostly empty." I handed her the popcorn.

"Sometimes I'm the only one here, but there are days when several others show up. I guess it depends on what mood people are in."

"How often do they do this?" I asked.

"Only once a month. But I try to come every time. My grandma was the one who got me hooked on these old movies. She used to bring me when I was younger."

"So in a way, this is your tribute to her."

"Exactly." She smiled.

"Well, I'm glad you invited me then."

"Me too. Have you ever seen this movie before?"

"Can't say I have. I'm more of an action-packed kind of guy."

"Give it a chance. Let it speak to you. They don't make movies like this anymore."

"I'll do my best," I replied. I was pretty sure I was set for four hours of agony. I was already bored waiting for the opening credits to finish, but the picture finally started rolling, and the lead actress filled up the screen in her big white dress.

I leaned over to Nikki. "You're right. This movie is going to be awesome. She's hot. I'd totally date her."

She elbowed me in the ribs again and snorted in an irritated fashion.

I chuckled. "What? I'm being completely serious."

"You don't say things like that when you're with another girl. It's rude," she whispered.

"Oh. Sorry. What should I say? And why are we whispering? We're the only ones here."

"Quit talking and watch the movie," she hissed. "You're missing important stuff!"

"Yes ma'am. Forgive me for interrupting." I sat up rigidly in my seat, and she lifted a hand to her mouth trying to stifle a laugh.

I dutifully paid attention and found myself being sucked into the story. I kept glancing over at Nikki occasionally, enjoying her mesmerized look as she watched the movie. She was really into this. It was kind of cute.

Her hands were neatly folded in her lap, and I suddenly wanted to touch her. I boldly reached over and took the one closest to me, lacing my fingers through hers, resting them together on her thigh.

I didn't miss the small gasp she gave at my actions or the fact her hand was now trembling in mine. I leaned in next to her ear. "Relax, Nikki. I like you. Remember?"

She looked up at me and nodded. "I like you too."

I couldn't help the smile which broke across my face. "Good. Now we have that all settled, let's finish this. Okay?"

"Okay," she replied.

We stayed that way through the remainder of the show, me occasionally rubbing the back of her hand with my thumb, and once or twice she squeezed mine a little tighter in return. I didn't really concentrate on the rest of the story, but by the time we left, I was pretty sure *Gone with the Wind* was now my most favorite movie ever.

"Where to now, boss?" I was still holding onto her as we left the theater and headed toward my truck.

"I thought we could go to Sonic and get some ice cream, if you'd like."

"That sounds great." I helped her into the vehicle.

"Do you care if I plug my iPod in?" she asked when I got in on the other side.

"Of course not. Go right ahead." I rolled down my window to enjoy the nice air outside.

She took it out of her purse and hooked it up, getting it all situated as we turned into the drive in restaurant parking lot. I hit the edge of the sidewalk slightly when we entered and sent her bag flying to the floor, dumping its contents everywhere.

"Curb check," I called out. "Sorry."

"It's okay," she replied, bending over to pick up her stuff.

I pulled into a spot near the front. At that moment her iPod started blaring the song 'Barbie Girl' loudly through my speakers, for everyone to hear. I looked to see several guys from school I hung out with eating on the patio with a bunch of girls, staring at me curiously.

"Something you want to tell us, Walker?" Wes shouted, and everyone laughed.

I rolled my eyes and pointed in Nikki's direction, realizing then no one could see her since she was bent to gather her things.

"Sit up," I said abruptly, not wanting the guys to think I was jamming to sissy tunes.

She leaned over to grab a tube of lip-gloss which had rolled between my feet, and I saw we were in a suggestive predicament.

"Never mind. Don't get up," I amended quickly.

"What? Why?" She lifted her head to look at me.

I groaned as everyone outside saw her, and all of a sudden a bunch of catcalls and whistle's filled the air.

"Whoa ho! Look who's been lying in Walker's lap!" someone shouted.

Her face flushed red when she understood what everyone was thinking.

"Sorry," I apologized. "I tried to warn you."

"It's not your fault." She moved to the other side of the truck.

"Don't give them the satisfaction of looking guilty." I put my arm on the back of the seat and motioned for her to slide over.

She did so without hesitation, surprising me when she gave me a peck on the cheek.

"Thanks for trying to protect my reputation," she said sincerely.

"Anytime, and I mean it." I wrapped my arm around her shoulders and hugged her tightly.

~Chapter Seven~

I pulled up in front of her small but well-kept home and jumped out of the truck to open her door.

"Wow. I would've never pegged you as the gentlemanly type."

"I'm full of surprises," I said as we walked up the sidewalk together. "If you stick with me a little longer, you might even find out some more."

She paused on the porch. "We'll see." She smiled.

"Be careful. That sort of sounded promising. I'm starting to think I might get you to go out with me again."

"Hold that thought," she said, going into the house and leaving me standing there.

She reappeared a minute later, carrying a large, clear, glass vase full of water with a plant sitting in the top of it.

"This is for you." She handed it to me.

"What is it?" I asked, completely perplexed with this gift.

She laughed. "It's a betta fish. See." She pointed to the hanging roots.

Sure enough, there was a turquoise and purple fish with long, wavy fins hiding in there.

"It's pretty. Is it boy or a girl?"

"The pretty ones are always male."

"I guess that rules out naming it Nikki," I teased. "Not to seem ungrateful, but is there a reason why you're giving me this?"

She nodded. "There is actually."

"Are you going to tell me?" I asked when she didn't carry on.

"Keep both of them alive, and you can continue to date me." She looked up at me expectantly.

"So is this a test? You're seeing how responsible I am?"

She grinned. "Something like that, but I also thought you might enjoy it. They're fun to watch and talk to. I think there's something kind of soothing about it."

"Ah. I get it. It's therapy." I suddenly wondered if she saw me as a mercy date—the kid with problems who needed fixing. I didn't care for that.

"When my dad died, I went through a time when I felt as though I couldn't speak to anyone. It was hard for me to open up about things. We had a betta fish, and I started talking to it. It sounds silly, I know, but it helped me to air things out sometimes. I hope you won't think I'm trying to be intrusive. I thought I would share it, because it got me through a rough time."

I quickly reassessed the situation. She was honestly trying to help, and I really did want to date her. If that meant taking care of a fish, then so be it.

"Thank you. I know just where I'll put him in my bedroom." I smiled.

"Oh, one more thing before you go." She ran inside and quickly returned. "I forgot to give you his food."

"Yeah, it might help in the 'keeping alive' part." I set the vase and food down on the porch, before I stepped toward her. "I had fun today."

She wrapped her arms around me, laying her head against my chest.

I hugged her back, closing my eyes, as I smelled the sweet fragrance of her hair.

"I did too." She didn't let go right away, and we

swayed together in a natural rhythm for a moment.

"Do something with me next weekend too," I said, not wanting to release her, enjoying the sparks her touch was causing in my body.

She giggled. "If the fish is still alive."

"Then consider it a done deal, because I'll hire daycare for it if that's what it takes."

She laughed and pushed away. "I like you, Chase. You're funny."

"Really? I thought I was a punk."

"Yeah, you're that too." She winked, though, softening the blow. "See you soon . . . at school tomorrow." She stepped inside and closed the door.

Not soon enough, I thought.

I gathered my new pet and headed home.

My mom was surprised when I entered the house carrying my gift from Nikki. "Well, this is certainly interesting." She chuckled. "How'd it go?"

"It was great. We drove to California, went snorkeling, and made friends with some of the local sea life. I guess this little guy wanted to hang out longer." I smiled.

"Nice try," she said. "Only one problem with your story—this is a fresh water fish."

I shrugged. "I figured it was worth a shot."

"Seriously, how'd it go? I'm totally curious."

"It was fun, in a weird, trial sort of way."

"Trial?" she asked.

"I guess she was testing me to see how well I could handle difficult situations." I shook my head at the memories. "She took me to a rest home to meet her grandma, and then to the Silver Screen Sunday feature to watch *Gone with the Wind.*"

Mom snorted. "You went to watch that movie? I think I would've paid to see that."

"It wasn't half bad. Of course, we were the only people in the theater, and it was dark. Throw a cute girl into the mix, and it was kind of nice." I grinned.

She snickered. "I bet, but it still doesn't explain how you ended up with a fish."

"She gave it to me—told me she would date me as long as I could keep it, and the plant, alive. Apparently, she has the opinion I might be a bit irresponsible, though where she would come up with an idea like that is totally beyond me."

My mom rolled her eyes. "Yeah, I have no idea where she would've heard something like that. Are you going to keep it in your room?"

"Yep, on my nightstand, right next to my lamp." I turned toward the stairs.

"Take good care of it," Mom called after me. "And I want to meet this girl!"

"Okay," I replied over my shoulder. I entered my room and sat on the bed, placing my pet in its new home. I tapped the glass, trying to get the creature to pay attention to me, but it seemed more content to stay buried amongst the roots.

"So what shall I call you, little dude? I'm not big on what's popular in aquatic names these days."

Great, I thought. *I'm actually talking to a fish.*

I pondered ideas while I stared at it, taking in the beautiful purple and turquoise color.

"I think I'll call you Turk, short for turquoise. You okay with that?"

He didn't move.

"Last chance to object," I warned.

Still nothing.

"Then Turk it is. Welcome home, Turk." I lay back on my pillow and slid my hands behind my head, stretching out as I gazed at the ceiling.

Fish talking aside, today had been a pretty good

day—in fact, the best I'd had in long while. Things were definitely looking up.

Nikki seemed like a pretty cool chick. She definitely wasn't afraid to march to her own drum, but she was sweet and seemed genuine. While I knew she was different from the other girls I'd been with recently, I liked it.

I hadn't been on a real date since my dad died. Dating had pretty much consisted of going to a party and hooking up with someone there. While I didn't object to that either, I found I missed the structure of actually going out and doing something strictly to have fun and get to know someone.

Of course, I had no interest in knowing anybody before, so my lifestyle had worked for me. I wasn't even sure why I had the sudden desire to know Nikki. Something about her drew me to her, like a moth to the flame. I felt the need to connect to her.

"Get a grip, Walker," I groaned, shutting my eyes. There was no way I was turning into some girl's lovesick puppy.

Despite my resolve of the previous day, I found myself carefully scanning the parking lot for Nikki's car the next morning while I waited, casually leaning against the school.

"Hi, Chase," Brittney said with a smile and wave as she and Brett approached. I nodded and winked, giving her an admiring glance as she continued on into the building.

"Dude, your sister is freakin' hot. Why does she mess around with a jerk like that Matt guy?" I asked as Brett leaned against the wall next to me.

He shook his head. "I do *not* ask about her love life. That's something I don't need to know. Why do you care anyway? I thought you were all about Nikki."

"I am. I like Brittney, though. She's a nice girl. Matt doesn't seem to be the kind of guy who can appreciate nice."

"People say the same thing about you, bro. Heard you had a pretty exciting weekend, by the way."

"Meaning what exactly?" I asked, squinting.

"Rumor has it Nikki was getting pretty friendly with you in your truck."

I grunted. "You know what they say about rumors—they're rarely true."

"So you weren't getting lucky then?"

"Hardly. Her purse fell off the seat and spilled all over the floor. She was gathering her stuff."

"Man, that sucks. Maybe next time," Brett joked, making to fake punch me in the shoulder.

"I had fun with her the way things were," I replied with a scowl, wondering why I was suddenly feeling so defensive over the whole conversation. "I wouldn't change anything about how our date went."

"Is that so?" he asked, seeming genuinely surprised.

I nodded, staring back.

"Well, I guess what you say about rumors is true then, because the gossips say Chase Walker is a kid without morals. Now I'm a little curious about who you really are."

He honestly looked perplexed.

"That's the problem with most people I've met. They never take time to truly get to know a person before they judge them—myself included." I pushed away from the wall when I spied Nikki's car entering the lot. "Be careful with that curiosity thing too. It's what killed the cat." I chuckled as I moved past him.

I hopped off the curb, pausing for a second to allow a car to pass before I walked to where Nikki was parking. She waved through the window when she saw me approaching and grabbed her books in the seat next to her as she got out.

"Good morning," she said with a smile, and I reached around to shut the door behind her, glimpsing over her form. She looked amazing, as usual.

"Good morning to you too." I grabbed my cell phone from my pocket and flashed my screen at her. "I wanted to put your mind at ease right away. The plant— and Turk—are still alive today. I'd be happy to show you the time stamp on the image if you require proof."

She giggled. "Turk?"

"That's what I named him, short for Turquoise. He's a pretty cool dude. He yelled at me for sleeping in, but made up for it by helping me pick what to wear. How do I look?" I held my hands out, and she glanced from the ball cap on my head, over my clothes, down to the boots on my feet.

She swallowed thickly and flushed a bit.

"That good, huh?" I replied, pleased with my obvious effect on her. "I guess I'll have to keep Turk's advice then."

She shook her head. "You're a dork."

"You don't say?" I asked, taking her books, before I clasped her hand in my own. "I'm pretty sure that might be a step up from punk. Better watch it, Nikki. I'm really starting to think you like me."

She rolled her eyes and bumped her hip into mine. You need to get that wild imagination of yours under control. It might be bad for me to date a guy who takes tips on how to dress from a fish."

"No way. Turk has swag, and that's all that matters. You watch, he's going to be the next big thing in fashion."

We came to a sudden halt as Jeremy Winters squealed his jeep into the space right in front of us. He flashed an unconcerned look in our direction as Matt, another guy, and he jumped out.

"Dude, take it easy in the parking lot, would you?" I said casually as he walked up to us. "I just got Nikki here to go out with me. I'd kind of like to keep her alive a little longer."

I felt Nikki's grip tighten in mine, and I started to move past him, eager to get her away.

"Don't waste your time, bro. She doesn't put out, do you, Nikki?" Jeremy sneered, and Matt laughed.

A sudden rage pulsed through me. Without stopping to think, I dropped Nikki's books and swung around, punching Jeremy in the mouth as hard as I could. He staggered backward, grabbing his face before lowering his head and plowing into my midsection, sending us both sprawling onto the pavement. I quickly rolled over, straddling him as I pummeled him again. He landed a solid punch to my jaw, knocking me back a bit before I grabbed his wrists and pinned them beside his head.

"Anxious to head back to jail, Walker?" he panted, little drops of blood spraying from the cut on his lip as he spoke.

"Only if I get to take a dick like you with me." I leaned in closer. "I know what you did to Nikki, and I'd be more than happy to see you pay for it."

His glance darted to where Nikki stood with her eyes wide, tears showing.

Strong arms encircle my waist, dragging me away from Jeremy, and I struggled to go at him as he jumped up and ran for me again.

I saw Wes and Chad, run up to grab and hold him.

"He's not worth it, bro," Brett's voice whispered in my ear, and I realized he was the one restraining me.

Our actions had drawn a lot of attention without my notice. A large crowd of kids had gathered around us, and more were running in our direction. Brittney and Tana joined Nikki, towing her away from the two of us,

Matt following after them.

"Let me go, Brett," I said straining against him. "I'm okay. You're right, he isn't worth it."

Brett slowly released me, as if testing to see if I would jump to attack Jeremy again.

I bent to pick up Nikki's scattered books and papers, before going over to where she stood by the girls, frozen like she was in shock. I shouldered my way past Matt, who was glaring at me and seized her hand, pulling her after me as we began to weave our way through the other students.

"Did you see that?" someone whispered. "He kicked Jeremy Winter's butt."

"He deserved it if you ask me," someone else replied.

"Why'd you hit him?" another voice chimed in.

"He didn't like my shirt," I mumbled facetiously as I continued pushing past people.

I held onto Nikki even tighter and walked into the school, moving through the doors into the nearly empty library. I walked around behind a bookshelf, so we were out of the librarian's view. I set her books on the table.

"Are you okay?" I asked, nervous about how quiet she was.

"Me?" She stared incredulously. "I'm more worried about you. You're bleeding."

She touched the back of my arms near my elbows, and I noticed they were stinging. There was some slight road rash there from sliding on the pavement.

"I'm fine. This is nothing," I replied, shrugging it off.

"You might have a little swelling on your jaw too," she added, reaching to tenderly trace it.

I captured her hand and pulled it down. "I'm fine, Nikki," I emphasized again. "It's you I'm concerned about. I'm sorry I jumped him in front of you. He said that, and all I could see was him attacking you. I lost it. Who the hell does he think he is talking to you like this?"

My anger over the situation was rapidly growing again, and I wished I could've beat on him a while longer.

Nikki slid her arms around my waist and laid her head against my chest. "I've never had anyone stand up for me like that before. Thank you."

The frustration coursing through me melted away, and I naturally reached out to hug her tighter. "I'd do it again, anytime. I want you to know I'm here for you if you ever need it."

She chuckled quietly. "I think you've already proven that."

I lifted her chin with my finger. "I mean it—anytime."

"I know you do. Thank you." Her eyes were still brimming with tears, and I couldn't look away from them as I realized how close we were. Our faces were mere inches apart.

Involuntarily, I leaned in closer, and she swayed toward me.

"Chase Walker and Jeremy Winters, please report to the principal's office," a female voice blared through the school's intercom system.

The moment was broken, and I sighed loudly as Nikki stepped away from me with a concerned look. "Please don't tell anyone what he did to me," she pleaded. "I don't want anyone to know."

"Your secret is safe. I promise."

She held my gaze, and I stroked her cheek with my thumb.

"I'll talk to you later, okay?"

She nodded, and I turned toward the door.

"You might want to go home and change your shirt

too. It's ripped, and there are some blood spots on it."

I paused, trying to glance over my shoulder and see the tear she was referring to. "Man, Jeremy better watch his friggin' back because my fish is gonna be pissed."

Nikki choked back a laugh, and I smiled, happy to see her face light up again. I walked out and headed to the office.

~Chapter Eight~

"Do you two have anything to say for yourselves?" Mr. Woodside asked again, only to be greeted by silence once more.

"Jeremy?" he prodded further, trying to get to the bottom of what had happened.

"It really was just a misunderstanding," Jeremy supplied, seeming eager to not have me speak. "We've taken care of it between ourselves and moved on."

Stupid punk, I thought. If ever there was a kid deserving of the title, it was this guy.

"Well, I'm glad you seem to think everything has been resolved, but I need to remind you, fighting is not allowed on school grounds. You'll both be receiving detention. We're trying to teach the students here to strive for excellence, and frankly, the message the two of you sent today isn't acceptable."

"I'm totally fine with the detention," Jeremy said, sucking up further, making me want to sink my fist into his pansy wuss face one more time. I didn't think he could take another hit without breaking, though. His left eye was nearly swollen shut and turning a nasty shade of purple. His split bottom lip was quite large now—a dried trail of blood ran down his chin.

"And you, Mr. Walker?" Mr. Woodside directed his attention toward me.

"I'm good with whatever," I replied blandly, slouched in my chair like I had been since we entered, unlike Mr. Brownnoser sitting next to me, who was plainly doing his best to kiss up.

"Alright, Mr. Winters, you'll serve detention at lunch today. You're dismissed. Chase, I'd like to talk to you a little longer."

Jeremy threw a nervous glance in my direction, and I couldn't help the slight grin and cocked eyebrow I shot at him as he stood and left the room.

Mr. Woodside folded his hands on his desk and stared at me. "You were awfully quiet during all of that."

I shrugged. "Didn't have much to say."

"Did you start this fight?" he asked point blank.

"It depends on what you mean by started. If you mean did I throw the first punch, then yes. But only because he threw the rude comment that deserved it."

"Someone insulting you is not a valid reason to hit them."

I laughed cynically. "Is that what you think? He didn't insult me. He can try to slight me until he's blue in the face. I wouldn't give a crap. He attacked Nikki, though. I won't stand for that."

"Really? What did he say?"

I leaned to the side and chuckled wryly. "Does it matter? I know everyone around here thinks he's Boy Wonder in the flesh, but he's not. He's a jerk."

"It might help your case."

I shook my head in disgust. "He told me not to waste my time, that she didn't put out, and then he goaded her with his remark."

Mr. Woodside's eyes widened in surprise, and he pondered over this information for a moment before he spoke again.

"Okay, you'll get detention for throwing the first punch then, and that's all."

"I threw the last punch too," I added, feeling the need to let him know who had actually won.

He looked at me seriously. "Good," he said, and I

was the one who was shocked this time. "I think I successfully judged the winner by the damage you did to Jeremy's face. Don't get me wrong, I'm not condoning fighting by any means, but I felt he must've been the one who started it by the way he was so anxious to be cooperative."

I watched him with newfound respect as he began writing on a piece of paper. Maybe this guy wasn't so bad. He actually paid attention and listened to what people had to say.

"Here's an excuse for your tardy to class. I want you to serve detention in the after school session. I'll call your mom, or grandparents, and explain what happened and why you are going to be late. I don't want you and Jeremy in the same session." He slid the note across his desk toward me.

I took it, thinking my grandpa was going to freak when he heard about this, especially since everyone talked like Jeremy was the golden boy favorite of all the football coaches.

Mr. Woodside stood and walked to the door of his office, holding it open for me. "Try a little harder to keep your nose clean around here, okay."

I smiled and headed into the hall. I rounded the corner and found myself being roughly grabbed by my shirt.

"What did you tell him, loser?" Jeremy said, his face only two inches from mine.

I narrowed my eyes, instantly reverting back to the anger I'd felt earlier. "I told him you're a friggin' rapist who deserves to be locked away for life, and he should interview every girl you've ever dated to get the testimony of all those you've forced yourself on."

He blanched white.

I slammed my knee hard into his crotch.

He let go, flushing red, and fell to the floor,

writhing on his side in pain, as he clutched himself.

I knelt down, getting real close to his ear. "Hurts like hell, doesn't it? Do you know what they do to guys like you in prison? I think they'd love you—a lot."

His eyes burned with both pain and hate, but he didn't reply.

"If I hear of you doing this to any other girl, I'm gonna sing like a lark to any person who'll listen. You can say bye-bye to scholarships and college dreams and hello to a striped jumpsuit. And just in case you didn't get my message—stay away from Nikki. I don't want you to even look at her. Understand?"

He gave a barely perceptible nod.

"Good. Glad we're all straight now, buddy." I clapped him on the back. He groaned again, and I got up and left, feeling quite content about his current suffering.

I went to my truck before I headed back to class and reached into the rear seat for the backpack I'd gotten in the habit of carrying during some of my worst alcohol binging days. I'd occasionally need a change of clothes before returning home after a party.

I pulled off my shirt and quickly exchanged it for the spare one before going into the school again. I stopped by the bathroom, to check my face in the mirror, finding the slightly swollen, bruised area on my jawline. It smarted a bit still, but other than that everything looked good.

Turning on the sink, I washed the minor scrapes on my arms, only to be interrupted by the sound of someone puking in one of the stalls. I tore off some paper towels and was about to ask if the person was okay, when I recognized Jeremy's shoes under the door.

Sucks to be you, doesn't it? I thought, as I shook my head and left.

I was pretty sure I'd made a big enemy today, and I

was positive there were those who'd be happy to stand up for him too, if he ever decided to retaliate. I would definitely be smart to watch my back from now on.

I handed my note from Mr. Woodside to the teacher before I slid into my seat beside Brett.

"You survive?" he asked under his breath as he studied the lab printout in front of him.

"I'm fine," I replied, digging a pencil out of my binder and getting to work on the assignment. "Detention after school for throwing the first punch."

"What was the whole fight about anyway?"

"Nothing. Forget it, dude."

"Didn't look like nothing when I was pulling you off him," Brett said, sounding offended.

"I'll tell you about it later, okay? For now let's just say Jeremy decided he wanted a lesson in manners, and I considered it my civic duty to teach him."

He snorted. "He's needed that lesson for a while, I'd wager. Glad you could help him out. Maybe they'll let you count it as community service hours."

I laughed. "That would be nice. And it's a project I could really get behind."

He tried to hide his chuckle as the teacher glared at us. "I bet you could," he mumbled into his cupped hand.

We both worked diligently until the bell rang, giving us permission to escape from this prison into another one.

"What're you doing tonight?" Brett asked.

"Probably getting horsewhipped by my grandpa when he finds not only was I in a fight, but it was with Prince Charming too."

He grimaced. "Yeah, I don't think I'd want to trade places with you. I was gonna see if you wanted to hang out tonight. I scored a little blunt."

"Thanks for the offer, but if I'm to have any kind of

life in the near future, I'd better keep myself on the straight and narrow for a bit."

"I can see how that might be beneficial," Brett agreed.

"If I'm not grounded into the dust, maybe you can come over and play video games some night this week," I suggested. I didn't want him to think I was trying to avoid him.

"That sounds cool."

"Yeah, bring those losers, Wes, and Chad, with you too. We can have a little competition, and I'll see if I can coax my grandma into making us something great to eat."

"Okay, I'll tell them. Um, see you later," he added when he saw Nikki waiting for me at the door. "Hey, gorgeous." I sauntered up, quickly glancing around to see if anyone overheard. "I can call you gorgeous in public now, right?"

"Quit joking and tell me how much trouble you're in," she said worriedly.

"No trouble," I replied casually, and when she arched her eyebrow, I sighed. "Okay, after school detention. No big deal."

"And Jeremy?" She bit her lip.

"Lunch detention."

"So he got off easy too." She frowned.

"Not so much," I said with a shake of my head. "He's hurting in more ways than you can imagine right now."

"What do you mean?"

I gave her a half grin. "Don't worry about it, babe. Just trust I'll do whatever it takes to keep you safe."

She got this sudden look of adoration, and for some reason I had to fight back a moment of panic.

I was plainly growing way too attached to this girl, making outlandish promises and such. It almost seemed as if fate was determined to twist our lives together. My old fears rose up and hit me hard. Suddenly, I didn't know if I was ready to care this much about someone again.

I coughed and moved, trying to distance myself from the emotions she was causing me to feel.

"Gotta go, or I'm gonna be late. Can't afford another detention now, can I?" I spun away, but not before I noticed her confusion.

During my next period, I tried to ignore the hammering staccato rhythm that seemed to pound the word "jerk" over and over into my mind, but it was so loud I could hardly concentrate. The teacher called on me to read a piece in the Iliad, and it was as if I couldn't even understand the English language anymore. I was so distracted.

"Winters must've hit him harder than we thought," a sardonic voice floated up from behind me, followed by some twittering laughter through the rest of the class. I didn't even bother checking to see who had said it. Honestly, I didn't give a crap what anyone else thought about me. What reason was there to try and please people, when they were clearly going to draw their own opinions of who I was, regardless of what I did?

I stumbled my way through the rest of the piece, and then slumped into my chair when I was finished. I didn't hear anything said for the rest of the class. I could only see Nikki's face floating in front of me, torturing me with her parting expression.

I watched the clock tick away every second of the remainder of the hour, springing to my feet when the bell rang and hurrying out the door ahead of everyone. Searching the locker hall, I looked around for Nikki, but didn't see her anywhere. I walked toward her next room, hoping to catch her and apologize, but couldn't find her.

Lunch arrived, but I still hadn't seen her. I was starting to get worried because it seemed Jeremy had mysteriously disappeared too. All of a sudden, unbidden thoughts of terror coursed through me. He wouldn't really try to hurt her after I'd threatened him with going to the police, would he?

"Dude, what is up with you?" Brett asked. "You're acting weird."

"Have you seen Jeremy since this morning?" I replied, still scanning the hall.

"Yeah, he went home after third period. His dad came and got him because he was feeling too sick to drive. I think you worked him over more than you realized." He clapped me on the shoulder. "Mr. Tough Guy, that's what we should call you from now on." He laughed. "Why do you want to talk to him anyway?"

"I don't," I answered with a shake of my head, as I spied Tana talking to Brittney. "Hang on a sec, bro."

I hurried over, causing Tana to look up in surprise when I grabbed her arm roughly, twirling her to face me. "Where's Nikki?" I asked abruptly.

"Uh, hello. You're hurting me," she said with a frown as she wrenched her arm away.

"Oh, sorry. I didn't mean to." I took a step back, glancing between both the girls. "I'm just worried. I haven't been able to find Nikki. I wanted to make sure she was okay."

"Her little sister got sick at school. She had to go pick her up and stay with her because their mom wasn't able to get off work," Brittney spoke up.

Tana gave me a strange look. "You have her number. Why didn't you text her yourself?"

Relief coursed through me, as well as a moment of feeling stupid. "I thought I might've hurt her feelings earlier. I didn't know if she was avoiding me on purpose."

Tana shrugged. "Well, if you did she certainly didn't say anything to me about it. All I ever hear lately is her singing your praises."

"Thanks, Tana." I grinned. "It's nice to know all my charm is finally working. I needed to hear that."

"Well, don't tell her I told you."

"It was a nice thing you did today, by the way," Brittney said.

I narrowed my eyes, wondering if she was being serious. "I think your boyfriend would beg to differ."

She shrugged. "I don't care what he thinks. Jeremy can be a real loser, and it's about time someone called him out. I wish Matt would learn to stand up to him too."

"I don't know... can you teach a pansy new tricks?" I gave her a questioning look, and she punched me in the arm.

"You don't like him. How come?"

I shook my head. "I think you could do better. I've got to go get hold of Nikki now. Have a nice day ladies."

"Everything all right?" Brett asked when I rejoined him.

"I think so. I need to check one more thing."

I dialed Nikki's number.

She answered on the second ring. "Hey."

"Hey, yourself. You doing okay?"

"Yeah," she replied, basically repeating the same story I'd just heard. "I was getting ready to text you while you were out for lunch."

"Okay, I was worried about you. I thought you'd been kidnapped or something. Kind of went frantic on everyone."

She laughed. "You're such a tease."

"I'm dead serious. Can I come see you after my detention this afternoon?"

"Sure. Come on over."

"Alright. I'll catch you later then," I replied, hanging up the phone and turning to Brett. "Let's go eat."

~Chapter Nine~

After serving my time at school without further incident, I pulled up in front of Nikki's house and sat staring at it. I needed to apologize for my earlier behavior and running away from her like I did.

It was time to face the music. I liked her a lot, and that was okay. It wasn't as if I had to be committed for the rest of eternity. I could just relax, see where things went naturally, and have some fun along the way.

I climbed out and headed toward the door. Nikki opened it before I could knock, lifting her finger to her lips.

"My brother and sister are sleeping. Clara's sick, and Timmy fell asleep beside her when he got home from school." She stepped aside and gestured for me to come in, closing the door behind me.

"How old are they?" I asked staring at where they lay snuggled on the sofa together.

"Clara is seven and Timmy is five. She's in second grade and he's in all-day kindergarten. They're best friends, though, and rarely ever this quiet, so I'm determined to enjoy it."

"Gotcha." I totally understood how that might be nice. I didn't have any siblings, but I had enough cousins to know kids this age could get rowdy.

"So what's up?" she said after a slightly awkward pause. "Did you come over for some reason in particular?

Leave it to Nikki to be so direct it made me nervous.

"Uh, yeah . . . I guess." I slid my hands into my pockets, glancing down at my shoes for a moment while I tried to compose myself. "I wanted to apologize for being a jerk and ducking out on you earlier today."

"Yeah, I noticed. Why did you?"

Okay, so she wasn't going to go easy on me.

"I just had a moment of panic, but I'm better now."

"Panic over what?"

Damn. She was going to make me spell it out.

"Over how much I like you," I replied honestly, and she made a little "oh" shape with her mouth, but no sound came out. "I didn't mean to, you know."

"Mean to like me so much?" she asked for clarification.

"Yeah. Getting close to someone again hasn't really been a top priority of mine."

"I see," she answered, but she still had this wrinkle of concern on her brow. "So what are you going to do about it?"

"Nothing." I sighed. "I'm gonna quit fighting everything and let life take me wherever it wants."

She placed her hand on my chest. "Chase, this is your life. Only you can decide what it's going to be like. It can be anything you want it to be, but you have the power to steer your ship where you want it to go."

"Is that so?"

"It is if you believe it. What do you want?"

I stepped closer, wrapping my arm around her waist and dragging her up against me. I gazed down into her big brown eyes, wondering if she could feel my heart pounding in my chest.

"Kiss her," a soft voice came from the couch, and I turned in surprise to find Clara staring at us with sleepy eyes and a grin.

Nikki blushed heavily. "I'm sorry, the kids get excited, and they say dumb—"

I silenced her by covering my mouth over hers. Her body felt so good as it melted into mine, her arms reaching up to intertwine around my neck, and she kissed me back.

I couldn't help myself as I deepened the contact, slipping my tongue between her lips to taste her for the first time, and sparks raced through me.

Suddenly, I felt like I couldn't get enough, and I caressed her urgently, running one of my hands up into her hair, pushing her face harder to mine. I couldn't ever remember being affected so much by such a simple touch.

Another child-like giggle brought us both back to reality, and Nikki gasped as we broke away from each other. I found myself slightly out of breath, as I looked between her and her little sister.

"Sorry. I didn't mean to get so carried away," I apologized.

She waved her hand away as if it was nothing, but the color of her skin said otherwise.

"Clara, go back to sleep so you can get feeling better." She tucked the blanket up higher under the young girl's chin.

"He's cute," Clara said dreamily and closed her eyes. It wasn't long before her breathing was deep and even again.

"Would you like a drink?" Nikki said, walking past me into the hallway.

I followed into the kitchen, leaning up against the fridge and watching her as she moved about the space, stretching to reach into the cupboard. I couldn't stop thinking about the way she felt in my arms, as she filled the glass and turned to give it to me. I took a couple of quick swallows before setting it down on the counter.

"Come here," I said, holding my hand out, and she took it without hesitation. I pulled her into my arms, and she laid her head against my chest. We fell into this natural swaying rhythm as we cuddled together, and I found myself wanting to keep her close.

She eventually slid from my grasp, mumbling something about needing to check on the kids, and I followed her into the hallway. She peeked briefly around the corner.

"Good they're still asleep. My mom's going to hate me for letting them nap so long, because they probably won't rest well tonight now." She stepped toward the doorway once more. "Would you like to squeeze into the recliner with me and watch some television?"

I grabbed her before she got too far away and spun her around, pressing her body up against the wall with my own. "I'd rather pick up where we left off, if you don't mind."

"I don't mind." She tilted her head, and I lowered my face to hers again.

The same shock rushed through me once more, setting my body aflame. I couldn't believe the electricity moving between us, more powerful than anything I'd ever experienced before. Her lips were so soft and yielding under my own. I couldn't seem to get enough. I pressed against them, teasing with my tongue and even nibbled with my teeth.

She made a happy little sighing sound in the back of her throat, and I started chuckling into her mouth before I broke away slightly.

"You enjoying yourself?" I asked, nudging her nose with my own.

"Very much. And you?" She smiled, her stare never leaving my mouth.

"It's okay," I replied, and her gaze flashed up to lock with mine.

"Only okay?" She looked truly worried.

"Alright. It's a little more than okay."

She bit her lip before she pushed me away. I was about to protest when she grabbed my hand and pulled me through a nearby door.

"This is my room."

It wasn't big, but it was well cared for. The furnishings were made of a painted black wood and consisted of a twin-size bed, dresser, desk, and ceiling-to-floor bookshelves. Her bed was covered in a white bedspread and pillows which matched the curtains at the window. There was an overstuffed white chair and ottoman pushed into a corner as well.

"So you like to read," I observed, as I ran my fingers over some of her titles.

"Yep. I'm a big romance fan, in case you couldn't tell. And I love pretty much all things paranormal."

"Really? So you're into the whole vampire craze?"

"Absolutely." She grinned. "There's nothing better than a good bite."

"Is that how it is?" I yanked her to me and leaned in to nip her neck, and she squealed. "Like this?" I breathed against her, and she shivered, as goose bumps rose over her skin.

"Something like that," she whispered breathlessly.

She smelled so good, I didn't want to move. She held still as I brushed my lips up the side of her neck and face until I found hers again. I feathered a light kiss over her mouth before I reached down and swung her into my arms.

"I thought romance heroes swept their girls off their feet and carried them off to bed." I chuckled evilly at her shocked expression which turned to delight when I stepped over to deposit her on the soft mattress with a bounce.

She giggled, and an elated look passed across her face as she scooted over and patted the spot next to her. "Are you going to join me?"

"What kind of hero would I be if I didn't?"

"A virtuous one perhaps? Or one who is great at resisting temptation?" she teased.

I appeared to ponder this for a moment. "No, I can safely say neither of those descriptions have ever applied to me. Sorry."

She shrugged, as I sat next to her. "Okay. I guess I'll have to settle for whatever you've got."

"Hey now," I said, rolling over and pinning her under me. "Be nice, or I may have to torture you instead." I laughed and started tickling her. She squirmed and thrashed beneath me, trying to get away. "Give up yet?" I asked.

"Never!" She grabbed me, smashing her lips to mine.

Something ignited, racing through me at the contact, and I groaned as I pressed against her, feeling every part of her body connected with mine. Her tongue invaded, causing a burst of pleasure to course through me at her aggressiveness.

I tried desperately to hold myself in check and kiss her slowly, but she clutched at me urgently. I easily moved from her lips, to her neck, and down to the exposed skin under her throat. I was completely on fire for this girl, and I didn't want to stop, but my brain was screaming warnings to put the brakes on before we reached a point where we couldn't turn back.

"Nikki." I exhaled heavily, lifting away. "I need to go."

"I don't want you to," she complained, reaching up to kiss my neck as she wrapped her legs around my waist, keeping me anchored against her.

I groaned loudly. "I have to. Things are getting too crazy."

"That's okay," she replied, belying everything I'd ever heard about her.

I found her mouth again, delving into its sweetness, until I could barely breathe from kissing her so heavily. I wanted her badly—it would be so easy to take her right here, right now.

"I can't do this. Your mom could come home any second," I said, trying to douse the flames, knowing she would later regret anything that happened.

My every nerve protested as I sat up and untangled myself from her limbs, reminding me I always gave into my body's demands.

I climbed off the bed.

"Please stay, Chase."

It took all I had to keep from crawling right back up there with her.

I swallowed hard. "You're babysitting, remember?" I was grasping at straws.

"Oh," she said, crestfallen. "I didn't think about that."

I smiled and took another step backward toward the door. "That's the problem. Neither of us are thinking right now."

She gave me a slight nod and continued to stare. Her swollen lips and messed up hair beckoned to me.

"Thanks for letting me come over," I said lamely. "I'll call you later. I hope your sister feels better soon."

I turned and fled from the house as quickly as I could, climbing into my truck and practically squealing out of the driveway in my eagerness to put some distance between us.

Admit it, Walker. You have it bad for this girl, I thought.

I'd never walked away from a willing partner before, and most definitely not because I wanted to protect her feelings and virtue.

I felt like I was losing my mind.

~Chapter Ten~

One cold shower and a brief nap later, I woke to the buzzing of my phone.

"Hello?" I answered groggily.

"Are we okay?" Nikki asked, sounding worried. "You never called."

"Sorry. I fell asleep." I swear my traitorous body was excited just to hear the sound of her voice. "Yeah, we're good. At least I think we are. Is there something you wanted to talk about?"

"I wanted to apologize. I've never attacked anybody like that before."

I grinned. "So, I'm the first? I feel honored."

"Quit teasing me. I'm being serious."

"So am I. You don't have anything to feel sorry about. I had fun. Way too much fun, as a matter of fact."

"Why did you leave then?"

"Because I didn't want to rush into something you weren't ready for. It's hard to make a rational decision when you're in the heat of the moment."

"I get that, but why did you have to leave? We could've hung out and visited together."

I laughed. "If I would've stayed one more minute, there would've been no stopping us. I wasn't leaving because I didn't want to be with you. Trust me. I love every second I spend with you."

"Well, you know what I learned today?"

"No, tell me."

"Chase Walker isn't the player everyone says he is."

I paused for a moment, dragging my hand through my hair. "Yes, I am, Nikki. At least I was. I'm different with you for some reason."

"Oh."

I heard a vehicle and rolled over to check out the window. "Hey, my grandpa is home. I'm gonna have to go now. I'll talk to you tomorrow at school, okay?"

"Alright." She paused for a second. "Have a good night."

"You too." I snapped the phone shut and reached for my shoes.

I hadn't got the horse stalls cleaned yet today, and I was pretty sure Grandpa had heard about my fight at school by now. He wasn't going to be very happy with me, of this I was positive.

Mom left me a note when I got home, stating Grandma had gone with her to show a house in a neighboring town, and they wouldn't be home until later, so there wasn't even anyone to run interference.

His heavy footfalls greeted me as I left my room. I met him in the hallway. If the scowl on his face were any indication of my current situation, things were not good.

"I need your help in the barn," he said gruffly.

"Headed that way now," I replied. "I fell asleep after school before I got my chores done."

He gave a grunt, casting his gaze over me once before he turned to go back down the stairs. I followed after, keeping up with his long stride until we entered the barn, and I went to get some of my supplies.

"I need you in the hayloft for a minute," Grandpa said as he started to agilely climb the ladder.

I placed the shovel I was holding against the wall and followed him up into the loft in time to see him open the exterior door. Light from the dusky sky filtered into the space, and for a moment, we stood there in silence as we stared at the scenery.

"Pretty sight, isn't it? Great view," he spoke softly.

I nodded. "I'd have to agree." I was a little shocked to find I meant it too. There was a certain peacefulness to this place.

"Do you know how hard I've worked to build this ranch? How I struggled to carve a successful niche for myself and my family—your family?"

I wondered where this line of questioning was going. "No sir, I don't. But I'm sure you could tell me all about it." I was completely serious.

"What I don't understand about you, kid, is how you could have such a blatant disrespect for another's property?" He gave me a hard look, flexing his jaw tightly. "Does it mean nothing to you that your whole family has shifted their entire lives to accommodate a better one for you? Are you really that selfish?"

I was lost. I'd been expecting a lecture about fighting, and he had thrown me by going off on a completely different tangent.

"I'm sorry, but I honestly have no idea what you're talking about. Of course I appreciate what everyone tries to do for me. I may not agree with what those things are, but I'm not totally insensitive."

"Is that so?" he countered. "Then perhaps you would care to explain these burn marks I found on the floor here." He stamped his booted foot in emphasis, drawing my attention to the area he was speaking of.

Swallowing hard, I cast my gaze back outside, searching frantically for some excuse to cover up what I'd been doing. Nothing came to mind, though, so I chose to stay silent.

"Don't think for one second that not saying anything is going to keep you safe." He reached into his pocket and pulled out the paper butt end of a joint. "I know exactly what you've been doing up here."

My stare was transfixed on the object in his hand, wondering how I'd been so unthinking as to leave such evidence behind.

"Smoking? In a hayloft?" his voice thundered. "You do have enough brains in that head of yours to realize you could've burned the whole place—with all the livestock inside of it—to the ground, don't you?"

Again I didn't reply. He was angry and rightly so. I'd been careless and stupid, even if it wasn't intentional.

"Don't you have anything to say?" he demanded.

I shook my head. "Nothing that'll improve the situation."

He grunted in disbelief and walked a couple steps away before swinging around. "How about I'm sorry? Did that ever cross through your thick skull?"

"Would you believe me if I said it?" I snapped back. "Because as far as I can tell, everyone in this whole damn place has already passed judgment on me and the kind of person I am!"

"That's because you never give anyone a chance to believe otherwise!" he hollered. "You're a complete disgrace to the memory of your father!"

His words slammed into me so hard I physically staggered backward, but if he noticed he didn't care, continuing on.

"I think he would cringe in horror if he could see the person you are now. You've turned into the one thing he always tried to prevent, an unimpressive kid with no sense of direction in his life. Why do you think he always pushed you so hard in school and sports? He wanted you to succeed—to make something of yourself! Instead you've taken his memory and used it to become a drug addict, an abuser of yourself and the people around you. I can't work with a kid who has no respect for himself or anyone else."

I was seething, feeling the rage build inside so hotly all I could see was red. "You don't know anything about me," I spat out.

"Is that so? Then if you're so wonderful, why don't you explain why you beat the crap out of a guy who *is* going places, in the middle of the parking lot at school? Feeling a little jealous of him already, are you?"

Fury welled, coursing through my body. "You might want to get your golden boy facts straight before you start accusing me of anything, because if that bastard ever messes with me again, I'll give him worse than he got this time."

"No. You listen to me. If you don't start following my rules right this minute, then you're going to be looking for a new place to live. And that means no more fighting, smoking, or drinking! Do you hear me, kid?"

"I'm not your kid. Let me save you the trouble of kicking me out." I pushed past him and practically slid down the ladder in my hurry to get out of there. I stormed off to the house.

I ran into my bedroom and started throwing my things into a duffle bag. I glanced around one last time, and landed on the vase on my nightstand. I grabbed it too, heading out to my truck.

Grandpa stood with his hands on his hips in the entrance of the barn. "Where do you think you're going?"

"Anywhere that isn't here will be fine," I shouted. I tossed the bag into the rear seat of the truck. "Be sure to tell my mom I love her when you fill her in on what a horrible *kid* I am."

I climbed inside placing the fish carefully in between my legs to keep it steady, and I left, pressing past the desire to peel out of the driveway like a madman. I felt like Grandpa's stare was burning a hole into the back of my head until I was finally out of view.

The words he said to me reverberated off my chest, repeating over and over as my heart bled. "You're a complete disgrace to the memory of your father." They hammered into me, opening all those wounds I'd so carefully tried to stitch closed. Everything inside me felt fresh and raw, as if my very skin had been ripped from my body to expose all that lay beneath.

Hot tears streamed down my face. I didn't want them, but they were unstoppable as my thoughts and feelings jumbled together in an overwhelming mass. I had no idea where I was going, and was surprised when I found myself parking across the street from Nikki's house—no memory of making the conscious decision to go there.

I didn't get out of the truck, though. I moved the fish to a smooth spot on the floorboard and leaned over the steering wheel onto my arms while I tried to get control. I had no idea how long I'd been sitting there, when I heard the passenger door open.

"Are you going to sit here all night, or are you actually going to come in?" Nikki laughed.

I couldn't look at her. Even though it was mostly dark, I didn't want her to see me like this.

"Chase?" she prompted, concern laced through her voice now.

When I didn't answer, she slid inside and closed the door.

"What's wrong? Did something happen?"

Suddenly, I simply wanted her to be there for me. I needed to know somebody was on my side, no matter what. I turned toward her in the dim glow coming from the streetlight, thinking I must truly look a mess when she gasped.

"It went bad with your Grandpa, didn't it?" she

asked.

The fact she could so easily decipher what was wrong, endeared her to me even more. I moved over, laying my head on her lap, hating that I felt so moody and vulnerable. She didn't ask me to explain—instead she ran her fingers through my hair, stroking it in a comforting manner. I closed my eyes and tried to concentrate solely on the sensation, attempting to push the anger from my mind.

I stayed there for several minutes before I finally felt calm enough to talk, but when I sat up and glanced at her sympathetic face, my heart went out to her. She was clearly upset, but patiently waited for me to address her. I just wanted to kiss her, though. I slid my hands up into her hair, holding her as I pressed my mouth to hers hard.

This girl was unique, different, but in a good way. She had her own scars and baggage, but she'd put them aside to get to know me. I hadn't been around her very long, but somehow she seemed exactly like the person I needed—the person who would stand beside me, because she wanted to.

"Chase," she said, pushing away slightly. "Are you okay?"

I sighed and leaned back against the seat. "We argued, and he threatened to kick me out. I packed up some of my things and left."

"Wow." She looked shocked. "What are you going to do?"

I laughed wryly. "I have no idea. I have a little money. I saved everything I earned from when I worked, and my dad would match all I made plus some. But it's not enough to go rent a place indefinitely or anything. Staying at a hotel would eat most of it up in a couple of weeks, especially by the time I added in food and stuff."

"I can't believe he was so upset about your fight," she said, shaking her head. "Didn't he realize Jeremy was the jerk who started it all?"

"It wasn't just the fight. I didn't tell him why I fought with Jeremy either, since I didn't want to tell what happened to you. No, he was mad because he found out I'd been smoking in the hayloft." I rubbed my head in frustration. "He had every right to be angry. I was irresponsible, but when he brought up Jeremy, it all escalated through the roof."

"Oh, I see," Nikki replied, reaching to lace her fingers with mine. "Have you eaten dinner? Why don't you come in and talk to my mom. She's pretty good about helping out with things. I think you'll like her."

"I don't want to intrude. Plus, she doesn't even know me."

"She knows of you, and she's already aware you're here. Come in and meet her."

"Okay," I said hesitantly, but I had nowhere to go, so I figured why not? I started to follow her when I noticed my fish. "Hey. Can I bring Turk in?"

Nikki smiled. "Of course. He's already like family."

I grinned slightly. "I guess he is, huh? I hope you aren't going to hold it against me he's homeless now."

"You didn't leave him behind. That sounds pretty responsible to me."

I let out a sigh of relief. "Good. That takes a lot of worry off my mind."

"Give me the fish," she said, holding her arms out for it.

"Can't do that."

"Why not?" She looked perplexed.

"I haven't decided if you're cool enough to hang out with Turk. He's a special breed, you know. Very selective about who he allows into his inner circle." I cocked an eyebrow at her to see how she was taking the news.

"And how does one get into this exclusive group?" she asked, playing along.

"Well, you'll have to apply, I guess. Fill out a form. Pass an agility test." My gaze traveled over her very fit body. "You know the drill."

"Give me the fish." She yanked the vase from me, sloshing the water slightly.

"Hey! Take it easy. You're gonna scare Turk to death."

She rolled her eyes and turned to march up the sidewalk. "I don't hear him protesting much."

"Hmmm. He must've got a really good look at you and accepted you right away. I know I would."

"Guess you're smarter than you seem then."

"Oh, ho! I think I just got burned." I chuckled, and she joined in.

I opened the door, and held it so she could go inside, before I followed after.

A very attractive brunette woman with short hair was sitting on the couch, and I could tell immediately who Nikki got her good looks from. She was a younger replica of her mom.

"You must be Chase." She rose to greet me.

"Yes, ma'am." I reached to shake her hand. "Nice to meet you."

"Please, call me Justine. Nikki has told me so much about you."

"Well, that can't be too much in my favor, now can it?"

She laughed and squeezed my shoulder. "It's all about perspective, Chase. Sometimes evaluating things from different angles can shed light on a lot of things. Have you had any dinner?" she asked, abruptly changing the subject as she moved toward the kitchen. "I have lasagna getting ready to come out of the oven.

You're welcome to join us."

"Thanks. I'd like that." I didn't get a chance to say anything more because Clara and Timmy came screaming out of one of the bedrooms.

"Give it back!" Clara demanded.

"No. I want to play with it!" Timmy shouted, running down the hall and into his mother's outstretched arms.

"Kids, kids. No more fighting, or neither of you'll get to play with the toy. Besides, we have company and it's time for dinner."

Clara smiled widely. "It's the guy who was kissing Nikki! I'm glad you came again, because you're cute."

I coughed, trying to cover up the choking sound as I cast a glance between Nikki and her mom.

"Rule number one, Chase. There are no secrets in this house," Justine said.

"Understood," I replied, hoping Nikki wouldn't be in trouble.

Justine sighed, before turning to Nikki. "I remember what it was like when I kissed your dad back in high school. It was divine." She straightened and continued into the other room. "Long make outs in the dark, in his truck . . . ," she trailed off dreamily.

"Mom," Nikki said, dragging the word out. "You're embarrassing me."

Justine rolled her eyes. "Forgive me for being so uncool. I'm sure Chase gets it, though, don't you? You look like a guy who could appreciate a long make out."

I chuckled. I liked this lady. "I'm gonna plead the fifth on this one."

Nikki gave me a horrified glance from behind her mom as she sat Turk on the counter. I winked at her as she proceeded to help her mother gather some dishes and utensils for everyone before sitting down and gesturing for me to join her.

The food was delicious, and before long we were all talking comfortably together. I felt myself relaxing, but I should've known it wouldn't last forever.

"So, Chase. What brings you over here tonight?" Justine asked, casually redirecting the conversation back to me.

I cleared my throat nervously. "Umm, my grandpa and I had an argument tonight. I moved out."

Justine looked up at me abruptly with concern. "Where will you go?"

I laughed half-heartedly. "Well, I didn't really think that part through when I stormed off. I was kind of angry at the moment. I have some money, though, so maybe I'll get a hotel room for a few days until I can talk to my mom and try to figure something else out."

"You should move in with us and be our big brother," Clara said with a grin.

"Yeah! Live here," Timmy seconded.

"Thanks for the invitation," I spoke with a smile, and I reached to tousle his hair. "But I think your mom probably has enough mouths to feed right now without adding me into the mix. I'll still come by to visit if it's okay."

They both smiled happily, and I wondered if I would ever feel that carefree and trusting again.

"While it's true you can't live here, I don't see any problem with you staying the night. Nikki can sleep in my room with me, and you can have her room. It'll save you some money. Does your mom know you're here?"

I shook my head. "No, and I'm kind of surprised I haven't heard from her by now." I reached into my pocket and pulled out my cell. "Ah, it's dead. That's probably why."

"Here, you can use mine to let her know where you are," Nikki said, handing me hers.

"Thanks," I replied, quickly entering my mom's

number. I sent her a text telling her not to worry, I was at a friend's house, invited to spend the night. I also said I would call her in the morning when my phone was charged, but I'd rather not hash it all out with her tonight.

Nikki's phone buzzed almost immediately. R U sure you're okay? I've been frantic trying 2 reach U.

I'm fine, really. Just cooling off a bit.

That's good, and probably 4 the best. Grandpa is still pretty upset. Where R U?

At Nikki's house. Her mom offered 2 let me stay. Don't worry—everything is on the up & up. I'll introduce U 2 them later.

Ok. I want 2 hear from U first thing in the morning.

Ok. Love U.

Love U 2.

I handed the phone back to Nikki. "She says I can stay. My grandpa is still mad. I told her I would introduce you all to her."

"We would love that," Justine replied, scooting her chair away to take the dishes to the sink. "Do you have any of your things here with you?"

"Yeah, I do, out in my truck."

"Well, go grab them while Nikki and I clean up in here, and then we'll get you all settled."

"Sounds good," I replied. I couldn't believe how warm and friendly this family was. It was nice to be in a place that really felt like a home again.

~Chapter Eleven~

I finished brushing my teeth in the bathroom Nikki obviously shared with Clara and Timmy. At least I assumed that was the case, judging from the bucket of rubber ducks sitting near the tub. She didn't seem to be the type who would be playing with bath toys, but I had to admit that particular mental image brought a smile to my face.

"What are you grinning about?" Nikki's voice caught me off guard, and I glanced at her in the mirror before bending to rinse.

"Nothing you want to hear," I replied, watching as she started brushing. Even mundane tasks like this were a pleasure to participate in with her.

"You're still grinning," she spoke over a mouthful of toothpaste.

"You're fun to watch." I shrugged, folding my arms as I leaned against the wall. "Actually you caught me wondering if all these rubber ducks belong to you."

She chuckled and rinsed. "Yeah. It's a crazy fetish I have."

"Seriously?" I asked, unable to tell if she was teasing, and I was rewarded with an eye roll.

"They're Timmy's. He's the one with a serious duck obsession."

"Ah, good. I was starting to question your taste."

"I taste just fine." She grabbed my shirt and pulled me to her, kissing me on the lips, allowing her fresh, minty flavor to mingle with my own.

"Mmm. You do taste good," I added when she moved away.

I followed her across the hall into her room. The bedding had been turned down during my short absence from the space and the pillows fluffed.

"I hope you'll be comfortable in here. Is there anything you need? I've never had a boy spend the night before." She blushed.

"Well, I've never stayed in such a purely feminine bedroom before either, but I think I'm manly enough to pull it off." I yanked my shirt off and flopped onto her mattress, placing my arms behind my head. "What do you think?"

She swallowed thickly as she stared down my body before quickly returning her gaze to mine. "I think you're in no danger of having your manliness questioned."

It was wrong how much this girl could set me on fire. I got up and stalked toward her, grabbing her around the waist and hauling her next to me.

Her fingertips voluntarily slid up over my chest and wrapped around my neck.

"It's a pity you can't stay in here with me," I said, pushing a few strands of hair away from her features. I kissed her sweet tasting mouth one more time before taking her by the shoulders and pointing her in the direction of the door. "Now get out of here before your mom chases me off with a shotgun."

She laughed. "My mom doesn't own a shotgun."

"Oh, I'm sure she could find something suitable, if the situation warranted it."

Nikki cast a soft smile, her eyes trailing over my half-dressed form. "Then I guess I shouldn't tell you how good all those muscles look with your shirt off, should I?"

I shook my head. "No, you shouldn't. That could

turn out really bad."

"Goodnight, Chase."

"Pleasant dreams, Nikki," I replied as she closed the door. I stood there for a full minute, staring at it and wished I could go after her. I needed find a way to control these raging hormones of mine when I was around her.

"Sleep. I need sleep," I whispered, dragging my hand through my hair, letting out a deep breath and unfastening my pants. I left them in a heap in the floor, and slid in between the comfortable blankets, before turning off the bedside lamp.

Even with the room cast into darkness, I was on sensory overload. I could smell her perfume on the pillow, and it was intoxicating. Her sheets wrapped around me, brushing my skin the same as they would hers.

I groaned and hit the pillow with my fist. "Get a grip, Walker," I growled to myself, determined to think about something else.

My mind wandered to the fight I'd had earlier with my grandpa, and I wondered what I was going to do now. Surely my mom would understand I couldn't live like this anymore. This proved to be exactly the topic I needed, as I found my eyes growing heavy, and I drifted off to sleep.

"Chase."

I snuggled deeper into the covers.

"Chase," the familiar voice came again, along with a hand softly squeezing my shoulder.

I opened my eyes and blinked, wondering why Nikki was standing in my bedroom. I smiled and reached out, pulling her to lie beside me. The memories came flooding back now, and I remembered I was actually in her room. She wasn't an illusion.

"Hey sexy," I whispered into her ear, as I proceeded to nudge my nose against her neck.

She giggled and squirmed against me, and I liked it. But then she crawled off and put her hands on her hips, staring down with her head crowned in a glorious array of bedhead.

"You need to get up. Your grandpa's outside on the front porch. He wants to speak with you."

Her words effectively distinguished my playful mood. "What does he want?" I replied gruffly.

Nikki shifted nervously. "Please don't be angry with me for interfering, but I called your mom after you went to bed. I told her why you beat up Jeremy—the whole story, Chase, and suggested she tell your grandpa too."

I couldn't believe she'd put her neck out for me like that. I knew how badly she wanted to keep this to herself.

"Nikki, I don't even know what to say. You shouldn't have felt like you needed to expose yourself that way. I would've handled it."

"You fought him because you were defending my honor. I know your grandpa wasn't only angry about that, but I had to let them know what a good guy you are."

I threw the covers off, and moved toward her.

"You aren't dressed," she squeaked, blushing as I approached, and I stared down at my underwear-clad form.

"Sorry," I apologized, knowing I wasn't leaving much to her imagination now. "Habit." I hugged her, feeling her tremble in my arms. "I wanted to say thank you."

"You're welcome," she said, gazing up at me before she cast an anxious glance at the door. "You better get dressed. I need to start getting ready for school anyway."

I reluctantly released her and watched her scurry away before I grabbed my pants and t-shirt from the day before and slipped them on. I could hear noises, along with good smells, coming from the kitchen, but I headed in the other direction toward the front of the house.

Stepping outside, I found my grandpa sitting in the porch swing. I folded my arms across my chest and leaned against the railing, waiting.

He glanced over and let out a heavy sigh. "It appears I may have some apologizing to do this morning. When your mom filled me in on where you were, and what was going on, I thought I'd try to come and catch you before school."

I didn't say anything.

"Look, I'm sorry I lost my temper the way I did yesterday. I was really angry when I discovered you were still using marijuana, and then I heard about you being in a fight, and it all escalated from there. I didn't take the time to find out the facts first. I had no idea Jeremy was even capable of such behavior, and if I did, well, I would've kicked his butt myself."

It was difficult to keep the grin off my face from that mental image, so I looked away from him as I tried not to laugh.

"Here's the deal, Chase. I know there's a good kid inside of you—he's just a little mixed up right now and needs some direction. You've been a hard worker and done a good job at the chores I've given you. However, I won't tolerate you bringing illegal substances of any kind into my home. Period. So this is all up to you. You can quit with the dope and come back, or you can keep it up and stay gone. What's it going to be?"

I moved to sit on the steps to the sidewalk, trying to relax. I knew he wanted an answer from me right now, but I honestly didn't know what to say.

He didn't speak anymore either, as he waited, and it was a while before I decided to reply.

"This may all seem like a cut and dry easy choice to you, but it's not for me. Sometimes I get so caught up in everything it becomes painful. Smoking and drinking are the only things I've found to help numb the pain. I like it."

He left the swing and came to sit next to me. "But what are you really accomplishing? As soon as it wears off, you still have the same set of worries. You're using it as a coping mechanism instead of dealing with the real issues. You're adding to your own problems."

"That might be true, but for a few blessed hours I can forget. I need that."

"No, you don't. There are other ways of getting past old hurts. Move forward—make new friends, new memories. Find happy things to replace the old ones that aren't there anymore."

"Nothing will replace my dad," I said bitterly.

"Nothing should. But do you really think he would want you to sit around being miserable for him your whole life? I don't. He spent too much time trying to help you successfully build your future. Get away from self-medicating and come home. Coach Hardin will be starting early football training and weight lifting next week. That'll give you something new to focus your energies on." He paused for a moment to gesture over his shoulder. "And you've got a real pretty gal in there who seems to care a lot about you. Surely that can count as something good."

I nodded. "She's great. It's nice to have someone who isn't so quick to judge."

Grandpa gave a slight grimace. "Chase, I don't know what else to say except I truly feel I have your best interest at heart."

"Well, thanks for coming to tell me," I said,

standing up and going to the door.

"Will you come back home after school?"

I shrugged. "I guess there's a stronger possibility of that happening now than there was earlier. I don't know. I need to think some things over."

"Try not to be too long about it. Your mom might actually kill me if you don't show up soon." He stood and shook his head. "She was madder than a wet hen at me last night."

I wasn't entirely sure what the term meant, but I knew my mom never minced words when she was angry. "Tell her I love her, and I'll get hold of her soon. My phone is still dead since I forgot my charger."

Grandpa smiled. "Well, that's almost a guarantee you'll come home then, isn't it? I know how you kids can't live without your technological contraptions."

I had to fight to keep from rolling my eyes. "I've got to get ready for school, or I'm going to be late. I don't need another detention."

"Alright. Have a good day." He gave a slight wave before walking toward his truck. I didn't watch him any longer, instead going inside toward Nikki's room.

"Chase? Do you want some breakfast real quick before you shower? I've got cold cereal and hot blueberry muffins in here," Justine called from the kitchen.

"Sure. Sounds great. Thank you."

"Did everything go okay outside?" she asked casually as she brought me a bowl and spoon to the table.

"Yeah, it's fine. He apologized for a couple of things and gave me some advice."

"Well, if there is one thing I've always thought about Warren Johnson, it's that he's a fair man."

"So I've heard," I mumbled as I reached for the box of cereal, pouring it. Justine set the plate of muffins along with some butter down next to me.

"The others have already eaten. I need to go supervise the little ones getting dressed and fixing their hair. Are you going to be okay in here? Can I get you anything else?"

"No, I'm good. Thank you for everything, Mrs. Wagner. I really appreciate all you've done—especially with me being a complete stranger."

"You can thank my daughter for that. She's always been selective about who she trusts, and for some reason she trusts you. That's a big compliment."

I saw Nikki step out of the bathroom briefly—her wet hair wrapped in a towel—before she ducked into her bedroom. Even without her hair fixed and makeup on, she was still beautiful.

"Nikki's special anyway you look at it," I replied, lifting a bite to my mouth.

She slid into a seat. "You really like her a lot, don't you?" She stared directly at me as she awaited my answer.

I nodded and swallowed.

"Please be careful with her, Chase. Her heart has already been badly damaged once. I'd hate to see anything like that happen to her again."

"You have my word, Mrs. Wagner. I'd never intentionally do anything to hurt her."

"Justine," she corrected, patting my hand. "Call me Justine."

"Sorry," I smiled. "Old habit."

"Old is exactly how it makes me feel." She laughed as she stood. "I guess I better tend to these kids."

~Chapter Twelve~

Nikki rode to school with me, snuggled up against my side, and I liked having her there.

"You know it's actually a good thing for you I've been in so much trouble lately," I said, helping her from the vehicle.

"Really? Why's that?"

"Because you look so dang hot today, I'm totally tempted to kidnap you and go somewhere the two of us can be alone." I touched the end of her nose with my finger. "But that would definitely get me landed into more scalding water."

She laughed. "I figured you were probably sick of me by now. You know—staying at my house, sleeping in my bed, having to share the same bathroom."

"Nope. All those things make me want to steal you away even worse." She had no idea what her presence did, both calming and exciting me at the same time.

"I thought being around the little kids would've run you off for sure. They get so annoying sometimes."

"I like them. I think they're cute," I replied, reaching to carry her books.

"Which is proof you haven't been around them long enough." She laced her fingers through mine.

"You know you adore them. I can tell by watching you," I told her. "You're a good big sister. If you don't mind me asking, how come there is such a big age gap between all of you?"

She sighed. "Mom and Dad decided to have me not

long after they got married. Dad was diagnosed with cancer a couple of years later and was sick for a while, but then he went into remission, or so we thought. It came back, and he died two years after Timmy was born. I don't think Timmy even remembers much about him."

I squeezed her hand. "I'm sorry. I didn't mean to bring up a painful subject."

"No worries. We're learning to get by. We work together and try to stay busy filling our lives with new happy memories to go with the old ones we have of him."

I chuckled. "My grandpa said something similar to me this morning. Are you sure you weren't spying on us?"

She shook her head. "I'd never invade your privacy like that."

"Really? Aren't you the one who called my mom?" I teased.

"That was different," Nikki said, jumping to defend her actions. "I had pertinent information she needed."

"I'm not mad. I appreciate you trying to help out."

"Well, you stood up for me. It's only fair I do the same for you."

I stopped. "Is that the reason you did it? Because it was fair?" I didn't want her thinking I was some charity case.

"No. I did it because I like you, and I don't want you to end up living somewhere else away from here. I was afraid if you didn't go back to your grandparents' house then your mom might move you again."

Her comment struck me hard, because it made me realize how much I wanted to stay too. A couple of weeks ago, I would've done anything to escape this place. Now I'd do anything to stay. If I could adjust so easily to that, what else could I adjust to?

"Hey, you two," Brett's voice broke me from my reverie, and I turned to find him and Brittney walking behind us.

"How you doing, bro?" I asked as the four of us fell into step together. I flashed a smile over at Brittney.

"I'm good. Things go okay at home last night? I tried to call, but I couldn't get an answer."

"Sorry, my phone died. Things were rough, actually, but it's nothing that can't be worked out. So you've been checking up on me, huh?"

"Yeah, friends do that for each other occasionally, you know."

It suddenly occurred to me that's exactly what I had right here—friends—real friends who cared about what was going on with me when I wasn't with them. It didn't revolve around a party, or getting my next fix, or what I could do for them.

"Well, thanks for watching out for me. I'll ask my grandpa if you can come over tomorrow night if you like. We still need to have our video game competition."

"Sounds great," he replied, opening the door to school. "You want to come hang with us too, Nikki?"

"I don't know if I can. Cheer tryouts for next year start tomorrow." She glanced at Brittney. "Both of us will be busy the rest of the week."

"Dang! I knew I should've kidnapped you when I had the chance," I whispered into her ear. "Now I'm hardly going to see you."

"I promise I'll try to fit you in somewhere." She laughed.

"You better," I replied, bending to kiss the top of her head. "Or I'll have to come hunt you down."

As it turned out, my predictions for spending time together became entirely too true. I rarely saw Nikki over the rest of the week between my Grandpa working me to the bone to make up for my mistake and Nikki's demanding practice schedule. Our relationship was reduced to a few stolen kisses in the hallway between classes and late phone calls after mountains of homework to say goodnight to each other before the two of us collapsed into bed.

I was looking forward to my community service hours on Saturday, just so I could be next to her, even if it was only stapling papers. I missed her. I wanted to take her out that night, but Grandpa had designated it as the evening Brett could come over, and I didn't want to give him the brush off again.

But it didn't stop me from planning ahead. I'd found a sweet secluded place down by Silver Creek where the trees were big. Tall, green, natural grasses grew underneath them. It seemed like the perfect place to take Nikki for a picnic or something on a Sunday afternoon. My mind couldn't get over how nice it would be to lie on a blanket with her in the fresh, spring air.

I smiled when I felt my phone buzz in my pocket, knowing it was Nikki calling to tell me goodnight. "Hey sexy," I answered.

She laughed. "I hope you checked to make sure it was me before you replied."

"Nah, I know lots of sexy people. Figured it had to be one of you," I teased.

"Oh, so you have lots of girls calling you late at night. Is that what you're saying?"

"No, I'm saying Brett is sexy too and needs to hear it once in a while."

She snorted, and I chuckled. "That's such an attractive sound. Do it again."

"Not a chance," she replied, and I could still hear the humor in her voice.

"I wish I could see your face right now. We should download a video chat app," I suggested.

"My cell isn't as fancy as yours, remember? Only the bare necessities for me."

"Man, it's like you live in the dark ages, Nikki. How do you make it without playing video games on your phone? I'd probably go crazy on all my sports trips without something to do to pass the time."

"Girls aren't like that. We actually *talk* to each other on trips."

"Don't you mean *gossip*?" I goaded.

"Yeah, that too," she agreed with a slight giggle.

I flopped over onto my stomach and propped up on my elbows, waving my feet in the air behind me. "So tell me some great gossip," I said in my best feminine sounding voice. "I'm dying to hear everything you've been talking to people about."

"You're an idiot."

I could almost see the eye roll she was giving me right now, but she was laughing, and that's all I cared about. I loved the sound of it.

"I might be an idiot, but I'm your idiot."

"Are you?" she asked, suddenly serious.

"One hundred percent," I replied in the same tone. There was a pause between us as the words sunk in. I spoke up before she could analyze it too much farther. "I want to take you out on Sunday around noon. Are you up for it?"

"Sure. Let me ask my mom if it's okay."

I waited for a few moments before she spoke again. "She wants to know what we have planned."

"Can't tell you. It's a secret. If she really wants to know, then have her text me."

"Oh, so you'll tell her but not me?"

"Yep. That's how the secret thing works."

She disappeared for a minute again. "She says I can go if I help her get the house cleaned after I get back from working at the hospital."

"Awesome. I'll see you there tomorrow then."

"Great."

"Night, sexy."

She laughed again. "Night, stud muffin." She hung up before I could reply.

"Having fun there?" My mom's voice came from the doorway.

I turned to look and smiled. "I am, actually. Don't freak out when I say this, but I think I'm starting to like living here."

She walked in and sat next to me. "And if there wasn't a girl involved, would you feel the same way?"

I thought about it for a second. "I think so. I've made a few really cool friends, and from what everyone keeps telling me, the football team seems to have a pretty good program. I'm kind of looking forward to it."

"What about the jerk you got in the fight with? Is he still bothering you?"

"I've barely seen Jeremy since that day. Guess he took my warning to stay away seriously."

"I hope so, but I would watch your back anyway. You never know what will happen with someone like that."

"True." The conversation dwindled off for a moment, and I wondered when mom and I had grown so far apart it became difficult to talk to one another. I didn't like it.

"How's work going for you?" I asked in an attempt to keep things flowing.

"Wonderfully, actually. I sold a house, so I'll be getting a nice commission. I've also met some great people." She glanced away from me nervously.

"What kind of people?" I replied, feeling suspicious as I stared. I suddenly noticed she looked very dressed up, and she had this kind of glow about her.

"Well, there's this nice girl named Sarah who works

at the office. She introduced me to her brother last week."

She'd met a man. I felt a little sick.

"He's so sweet," she continued on. "His name is Greg Stanton, and he's a local contractor here in the area. He asked me out on a date for tomorrow night."

And there was the bomb I'd been waiting for.

"What did you say?"

"I told him yes." She looked straight at me. "I hope it's okay with you."

I couldn't help the sigh that escaped as I rolled back onto my pillow. "I don't know how I feel about it, Mom. I mean it's your life, and you should probably do what makes you happy, but I'm not gonna lie. It's weird to think of you dating someone who isn't Dad."

She laid her palm on my leg. "It's strange for me as well, Chase. I miss your dad a lot, but I've been really lonely. I know he hasn't even been dead for a year yet, so I understand if it feels too soon for you."

"It's been almost eight months. Seven months and thirteen days to be exact. If you want me to get really technical, I can probably give you the hours and minutes too."

My mom burst into tears, burying her face in her hands, and I felt like a heel. I sat up and wrapped my arms around her, letting her cry against my shoulder. She was sobbing uncontrollably, more than I'd ever seen her do since the day we found out he died.

"Mom. Mom, I'm sorry. I didn't mean to upset you so badly." I hugged her tighter.

"I know you didn't." She hiccupped. "It kills me to see how badly this has destroyed your life. I've felt totally helpless with no idea of how to reach you. Your dad was the one who always knew you best. He's the one I went to for advice when it came to you, and then he wasn't there. I feel like I let you down somehow. I didn't help you cope the way I should've, and so you turned to something else to try to find a way out. I'm certainly not going to be up for any parent of the year awards anytime soon."

"Is that what you think, Mom?" I said, moving to see her better. "You didn't make me this way. You were the stable thing in my life—the only person who was always there."

I felt a wave of emotions roll over me, and I rapidly took a breath, trying to push them away before I continued.

"I don't know how to talk about him without . . . without feeling like this." I gestured between the two of us. "There came a point where all I was doing was blinking back the tears threatening to overwhelm me. I couldn't take it anymore. I didn't want to feel it, so I chose the one thing I thought would help me forget— even if it was for a small while."

She nodded, showing she understood what I was saying and pulled a handkerchief out of her pocket, dabbing her eyes.

"Grandpa told me he found evidence you're still smoking pot."

I sighed—surprised it had taken this many days to bring up this conversation since I'd returned home. But things had been a little strained, so maybe she'd just been biding her time.

"I have once since we moved here, and I'd had a particularly rough day." I held up my hand to stop her when she opened her mouth. "I know. That's not an excuse. What I did was wrong, but I wanted to do it—so I did."

She reached out and rested her hand on my knee. "Sometimes we have to learn to be bigger than what we want, son."

"Easier said than done, Mom." I moved away,

reclining against my headboard.

"Are you going to keep using then?" she asked me point blank.

I shrugged. "Grandpa made it pretty clear if I ever did, and he found out about it, he would kick me out."

"That doesn't sound like much of a commitment to me." She frowned.

"Well, I know Nikki doesn't like it. She works for a drug abuse therapist."

"You need to quit because you want to, Chase, not because of someone else's opinion. Do you want to stop?"

I picked at an imaginary dust speck on my bedspread. "I want to stop hurting."

"That's what got you into this mess."

"I don't know what else I can give you right now, Mom. I'm trying, okay? I'm excited about things I haven't even thought about in the last several months. I look forward to different things every day. I even wake up happy sometimes. Am I healing? Maybe. Only time will tell, but I'm trying. It's all I've got at the moment."

"Then that's enough for me. Just keep thinking like that." She hugged me, and I slipped my arms around her. She gave a quick kiss on my cheek before she stood. "I love you. Don't forget that."

"Love you too," I said as she walked to the door. "Hey, Mom!" I called after her when she stepped into the hallway.

"Yes?" She reappeared with a questioning look

"This Greg guy . . . is he coming here to pick you up?"

She nodded.

"Where's he taking you?"

She smiled and crossed her arms. "Out to dinner. Why?"

"What time will you be home?"

She cocked an eyebrow. "Don't you even think about beginning to check up on me, young man."

"Someone's got to do it. It might as well be me. I need to make sure Greg knows who he's dealing with. No one messes with my mom."

Laughter bubbled up from inside her. "Put your swag away, Mr. Macho. I know how to handle myself without a little peon like you flitting about trying to ruffle everyone's feathers." She turned and walked away.

"That won't stop me!" I shouted, chuckling as I started to get ready for bed.

"It better!" she hollered back, surprising me.

I would definitely be here to check out this Greg fellow when he showed up tomorrow. She could count on that.

~Chapter Thirteen~

"You're late. You missed most of the group and left me to staple massive amounts of packets by myself." Nikki stood with her hands on her hips, glaring over me with disdain. "And you're absolutely filthy! What happened to you?"

"I hit some debris someone lost in the middle of the road. The rain was coming down so hard I didn't see it in time, and it punctured one of my tires. I've been putting the spare on and rolling around in all this lovely country mud you people keep up here."

I went into the bathroom and pulled a bunch of paper towels out of the dispenser and started wiping my face and arms down. I was drenched.

"You need to get something dry on. Why don't you go home? I'll explain what's going on to Maggie."

"I always carry spare clothes with me," I replied, nodding toward the backpack I'd tossed on the floor next to me.

She gave me a puzzled look. "You do?"

"While I'd love to tell you it's because I'm such a great Boy Scout, it's actually the product of waking up after vomit-inducing alcohol and drug binges," I explained.

Her eyes went wide.

"Give me a minute, and I'll get changed—unless you want to help me get out of these wet things," I added, lifting an eyebrow in suggestion.

"Shhh." Nikki blushed as she glanced around.

"Someone will hear you."

I shrugged. "So, who cares?"

"I do. They'll think we're . . . that we're . . ."

"That we're what?" I laughed, prodding her on. "Doing *it*? Weren't you the one who was begging me to stick around the other day?"

She gasped and shut the door much too loudly, closing me into the small space by myself. I couldn't help the grin that stayed on my lips. She was so fun to tease. I quickly changed and did the best I could to dry rub my hair into some semblance of order before I joined her.

"That looks much more comfortable." She shoved a stack of stapled papers in my arms. "Go pass these to the group out there while I set up some of the packets for next week."

"Yes, ma'am." I loved it when she was bossy.

I followed her instructions, slipping quietly into the room and waited for Maggie to give me the okay to start passing to everyone in attendance.

"Thank you, Chase," Maggie said when I was done.

"No problem." I headed back into where Nikki was working.

"I was wondering if you'd like to sit in on the group sometime?" Nikki asked, peeking over at me.

I came to a halt, her comment catching me completely off guard, and she hurried to continue.

"You don't have to talk if you don't want to. You can listen to the other's experiences and what they're doing to get past their addiction problems."

Moving to the table, I picked up the first few papers and began stapling them together. "I'm not addicted to anything." I knew I sounded short, but I couldn't help it.

"I'm not saying you are. I know you've used recently, though, and it's caused problems for you at home. I thought maybe you could learn some mental techniques—things to help talk yourself through situations when the urge comes up." She sighed heavily. "I'm sorry. This isn't coming out right. I know it's none of my business. I was trying to offer support—if you needed it."

I didn't answer, and to her credit, she didn't push the issue any further. We worked together in silence for quite a while until we had most of the work done for the next week.

She went to the water cooler and got a drink, sipping it while she watched me finish up the rest of the papers.

"I got plastered one night after my dad died," she said suddenly, capturing my attention. "I found the key to my parent's liquor cabinet, and I took three big bottles. I don't remember what they were now. I wasn't old enough to drive anywhere, so I went to this little meadow behind our house. I didn't like the taste of it, but people always talk about how great it is, so I figured it had to get better, right? I forced myself to drink it— guzzling until I was so sick I started vomiting everywhere. It was awful, and I felt worse afterward than I did before. I made up my mind I was never going to do anything like that again." She stopped and stared at me. "I just want you to know, even though my experience is different than yours, I get where you're coming from."

I nodded, going to her and reaching to stroke her cheek. She was so beautiful. I found it hard to relate her to the image of a young girl trying to binge it up in the forest. "I'm glad you were able to walk away from it. You were smart to do so."

"Are you going to? Walk away from it, I mean." Her warm eyes looked like melted honey as she stared into mine.

"I want to sometimes. Other times not so much." I continued to caress her face. "Does that bother you?"

"Yes, but only because I worry about you. I don't want something to happen that will end up hurting you even more." She closed her eyes and nuzzled into my palm. "I like you, Chase. A lot."

"I like you too, Nikki." I pulled her into my arms and hugged her tightly. "Thanks for the concern. I'll be fine. I promise."

"Then do one thing for me."

"What?"

"Take some of these worksheets home. You don't have to read them right away if you don't want to. But they're really good to help sort your thoughts and see certain patterns that trigger things. You can do the exercises and then set small goals for yourself after each one. People in the group who do them really like them. It's a great program." Her words came out in a nervous rush as she tried to convince me.

I sighed and released her. "Fine. I'll take them, but only if you agree to be my sponsor and let me call you at any hour of the day or night if I need you."

She didn't miss a beat, smiling as she practically skipped to the table to gather the information for me. She was so caught up in what she was doing, she didn't realize I'd extracted a reason to contact her at any moment.

I was going to use this to my full advantage.

"I'm so glad you said yes." She handed me a large manila envelope. "I honestly think it'll help."

I chuckled slightly at her obvious exuberance. "We'll see."

"Glad you finally made it here today, Chase," Maggie's voice broke in from the doorway. "I didn't think you were going to show."

"He got a flat tire in the storm," Nikki piped up

before I could answer.

"I'm sorry I was so late," I offered.

"Let me sign your community service hours off for you," she replied, waving her hand for them.

"It'll only be about forty-five minutes this time," I told her.

"Nonsense. You were trying to get here, and you still showed up even though you knew you'd missed most of it. I'll credit you for the two hours you were scheduled."

I wondered if she'd be so willing if she knew I'd come because I wanted to dally away every second I could with her hot assistant.

"Thanks," I said when she handed the paper back. I glanced at my phone. "I guess I better get going. I have a friend coming over, and I need to meet someone who's taking my mom on a date."

"All right. See you next week then," Maggie waved, dismissing me as she moved past me to the desk.

Nikki followed me to the office door. "Have fun with Brett tonight. I'll see you tomorrow."

"Sounds great." I leaned in to kiss her briefly on the lips, and I noticed Maggie's eyes shoot up in surprise. I guess she wasn't aware Nikki and I were dating now. "Later, ladies," I said and I left.

Video games were in full swing, blasting loudly through the surround sound speakers on the television system I'd insisted Mom keep when we moved here. She couldn't really argue with me since Dad and I had picked the equipment out together. Getting rid of it would be like throwing away some of his memories.

"Die suckers, die!" Brett shouted as we teamed up against the guys we were battling together online—Wes and Chad. It had been a pretty good match so far, but Brett and I had this in the bag.

My attention was suddenly diverted when my mom walked past wearing a short black cocktail dress which showed off her long legs in tall strappy heels. Her makeup and dark, honey-streaked hair was fixed perfectly.

She smiled. "How's the game going, guys?" she asked, continuing on her way.

Brett and I both looked down in time to see ourselves get blown to smithereens on the screen.

"Dude! Why didn't you tell me your mom was so smokin' hot?" Brett exclaimed as soon as she was out of earshot. "She's a ten for sure!"

I sent him a scathing glare as I tossed the controller onto the coffee table.

"Okay. Message received. Hot mom is off limits," Brett grumbled.

"What do you know about some guy named Greg Stanton?" I asked.

"Whoa, is that who she's going out with?"

I nodded. "Is that a good whoa, or a bad one?"

"The guy is loaded. He's a total workhorse—this big contractor guy. His house is the huge one in the middle of the country club, if you've ever been there. He built it for him and his fiancé, but she got this weird illness and ended up dying before they got married. He's been single all these years, living in that big old place by himself. Everyone says he'll never get over her. I've never seen him date anyone before."

So they had something in common, both suffering from extreme loss. I got up and moved toward the stairs.

"Have you ever heard anything bad about him?"

"Greg? Heck no! He's one of the nicest people I know—a really good guy."

While I was pretty sure I didn't want to find out my mom was going on a date with Jack the Ripper, I was fairly certain this news might be just as bad. I didn't want some Superman moving in to sweep her off her feet either. She and I were . . . well, we were a team, and we didn't need anyone else butting in as far as I was concerned.

The doorbell rang right as we hit the bottom stair, and a quick check through the window revealed a sweet, bright-red truck parked out in the driveway.

I heard voices coming from the direction of the kitchen, and Mom appeared with Grandma and Grandpa following after. She smoothed her dress down nervously as she walked toward the door, and I suddenly found myself wanting to throw a blanket around her so this guy couldn't look at her.

I stepped in front of everyone and opened the door a crack to find a tall, dark-haired man in a black suit on the porch with a handful of flowers. He was well-groomed and probably had a face women freaked over. I thought he actually looked a little like Superman, and I fought back a groan.

"Can I help you?" I drawled lazily, allowing him to see only me filling the gap in the entrance.

"Um, yeah. I'm Greg Stanton. I'm here to pick up Tori Walker. Is she ready?"

"Let me check," I said, shutting the door in his face. "You ready?" I asked, turning to look at Mom who was blushing.

"Don't be rude, Chase!" my grandma exclaimed as she rushed by, practically pushing me out of the way in her excitement. "Greg!" she said with a trill, welcoming him as if he were the greatest thing to ever walk on the planet. "Come in, come in. Yes, Tori *is* ready."

Greg stepped inside with a smile. "Thank you, Mrs. Johnson." He stopped short when he saw my mom waiting for him. He skimmed over her from head to toe and then back up again. "Wow. You look great, Tori."

I couldn't have rolled my eyes any farther. Maybe I should've handed him a spoon so he could continue to eat her up with his gaze.

"Thank you. So do you," she answered, coloring even more as she wrung her hands together.

They both stared at each other, and an awkward pause filled the air as we all waited for them to say something else.

"Give her the flowers, dude," I coached him finally, unable to take it any longer, and Greg sputtered to life as he peered down at the floral bouquet he'd obviously forgotten.

"Oh, yeah. Here, these are for you." He extended the gift, and Mom took them while she beamed.

"These are beautiful. Thank you."

"Let me put those in some water, dear," Grandma said, taking them and hurrying toward the kitchen.

"Greg," Grandpa stepped forward, smiling bigger than I'd ever seen him do. "Nice to see you."

"You too, Warren. How's the ranch doing?"

"It's all right. Getting everything ready for planting. Just went to Phoenix and bought me some new seeding equipment for the tractor. I'm looking forward to trying it out this next week."

Good gosh. Was this really what adult people talked about up here?

"Sounds great," Greg replied sincerely. "I hope it works well for you."

"Greg," my mom interrupted, moving beside me. "This is my son, Chase, I was telling you about."

"I kind of figured as much." Greg laughed. "He seemed like he was on watchdog mode. Way to keep an eye out for your mom, kiddo. Pleased to meet you." He extended his hand, and I eyed it warily before I took it, shaking it once.

"So, I hear Warren has been talking you up to

Coach Hardin for the quarterback spot."

He liked football, did he? Maybe there's hope for him after all, I thought.

"You're gonna have to work hard," he continued. "Jeremy Winters is leaving some big shoes for you to fill, isn't he, Brett?" he said, turning to clap him on the shoulder.

And all hope for Greg flew straight out the window.

Grandpa cleared his throat. "Don't be putting him off yet. I'd wager Chase's stats could beat Jeremy's any day. He's good."

I clenched my jaw to keep it from dropping in surprise at my grandpa's rapid defense. I had to get out of here. This was getting too bizarre.

"Nice to meet you, Greg," I said, stepping briskly past him. "Have a good time, Mom. Don't forget who you are," I added under my breath, and she laughed and blushed again.

I grabbed Brett by the arm, dragging him after me. "Come on. We've got people to kill upstairs."

"I think good ol' Greg boy has the major hots for your mom," Brett whispered as we made our way up.

"Shut up, man," I warned.

"Dude, I bet you end up with a new baby brother by next year," he prattled on, oblivious to my mood.

I swung around and faced him. "If you don't want me to knock that stupid head of yours right off your shoulders, then I suggest you shut it now."

Brett simply snorted. "Yeah. You saw it too, didn't you? That's why you're all worked up about it." He chuckled as he walked over to the couch and plopped down, picking up a controller. "I'm telling you, don't worry. This guy is the real deal, Chase. He'll treat your mom well." He chuckled again.

I heard the front door close, and I turned to look out the window, watching as Greg led my mom to his massive beast of a truck and helped her inside. I could hear her laughter tinkling through the air, and I felt slightly sick.

It should be my dad she's with, I thought bitterly.

I sighed and ran a hand through my hair. I wanted her to be happy again, I just wasn't sure I was ready for it to be this way.

~Chapter Fourteen~

"Where are you dragging me off to, Mr. Walker?" Nikki asked as she snuggled up closer. I loved the way her body brushed against mine as we bounced along the bumpy road in my truck.

I slid my arm around her tighter, kissing the top of her head. "I'm taking you into the middle of the woods so I can have my evil way with you. Haven't you figured that out already?"

She laughed nervously as she stared around outside the vehicle. "I'm actually starting to believe you, I think."

I glanced down and caught her eye. "Would it be such an awful thing?" I cocked my eyebrow.

She dropped her gaze and began toying with the bottom of her shirt. "I don't know," she hedged, and I felt bad for making her uncomfortable.

"Relax. We aren't far from the ranch house. In fact, when we stop, you'll be able to see the house over that rise. It seems far because the road swings in a wide circle before it comes around again. It only took me fifteen minutes to walk from there to here the other day."

"Oh," she replied, craning her neck in the direction I'd pointed. "Then why didn't we walk?"

"Because I had too much stuff to carry, and because everything is still a bit muddy after the freak rainstorm yesterday," I explained as I pulled up underneath the giant cottonwoods and parked.

"This is beautiful." Nikki's eyes were wide as she took in the creek running nearby and the tall grass blowing slightly in the spring breeze.

"I thought so too. Grandpa had me helping him gather some of the horses, and I came across this place."

I slid from the truck and reached into the bed in the back, pulling out a blanket and a basket full of food. "I thought we could have a picnic."

She grinned widely. "You packed us a lunch?"

"Oh, heck no. I wanted you to survive the date. My grandma made it."

Nikki giggled, and I handed the blanket to her so I could get the tarp I brought to go underneath it, in case the ground was still too wet.

"You ready?" I asked with a smile.

"Let's do this." She followed as I led the way to where the large branches of the trees intertwined heavily, creating a canopy of sorts that filtered the early May sunshine overhead.

"Does this look good?" I set the basket down.

She nodded. "It's great!"

I spread the small plastic and helped her lay the fluffy quilt over the top. We kicked our shoes off and settled into the center of our makeshift area.

"So what did you bring to eat?" Nikki asked, trying to peer into the basket after I placed it in the middle and lifted the lid.

"I have no idea, but there were good smells coming from the kitchen earlier, so it's bound to be awesome." I lifted a baggie with napkins, and a large plastic container. "Looks like fried chicken."

I passed it to Nikki while I got out a couple of plates and set them down. "And we have potato salad, as well as nacho flavored chips, and a container of mixed fruit."

"My mouth is watering," she said, and her comment

made mine do the same, for an entirely different reason.

"I can help you with that, you know." I captured her chin in my grasp and planted a kiss on her.

She sighed, and I chuckled when her stomach growled loudly.

"Okay, okay." I released her. "I get the message. I'll feed you first."

She blushed. "Sorry."

"Nothing to be sorry about."

We dished our food and dug in.

"Mmm, this is so good," Nikki groaned, mumbling over a mouthful of chicken.

"And greasy," I replied, handing her a napkin and taking one too. I found myself eating slowly, more intent on watching her, until she noticed my perusal.

"What?" She lifted the napkin to wipe her face. "Did I miss something?"

I shook my head. "Not at all. I just like how shiny your lips look while you're eating that."

"Be serious," she said, as she playfully pushed at my shoulder.

"I *am* being serious." I set my plate down before I tackled and tossed her back onto the blanket. "It's totally inviting."

I leaned my head in real close to hers, until we were only a hairsbreadth apart. "Did you get enough to eat?" I searched her eyes and she nodded. "Good." I closed the rest of the distance.

Her lips parted in invitation, and I took full advantage, sinking my tongue deep inside her mouth—stroking and tangling in the sweetness I found there.

"You taste so nice," I said, leaving to kiss her cheek.

"So do you." She lifted her fingers to trace around my mouth.

I captured one of them with my teeth and sucked on

it gently, teasing the tip of it with my tongue as I held it. She shut her eyes and a small sound escaped her lips—lips I had to devour again and again, until I slid to explore other locations. I moved to the hollow of her throat, nipping at her collarbone as I passed to place soft caresses against the skin exposed by the neckline of her shirt.

She arched against me, running her hands down my back, drawing me closer. Her light perfume filled my senses, driving me crazy with a desire for more.

"Nikki," I whispered, before sitting up slightly. My gaze moved down from her somewhat messy hair, to her swollen mouth, continuing to trail a path down her body, until it stopped where the hem of her shirt rested. It was pushed up a bit and revealing her belly button.

I couldn't resist and flashed a wicked look before I placed my lips there, feathering her with tiny, light pecks. She gasped in surprise, and a grin crossed my face. "You like that?" I spoke, blowing my warm breath over her.

"Yes."

I barely heard the word. I noticed she was trembling, and faint goose bumps rose on her flesh.

"Are you okay?" I looked up, seeing a moment of both fear and longing, followed by indecision, cross her features.

An image of that jerk, Jeremy, attacking her flashed through my mind.

I released a sigh and flopped over onto my side, propping my head up with my hand so I could continue to stare.

She was breathing heavily, and glanced at me with heavily lidded eyes. "Why'd you stop?" she asked.

"Because you're nervous, and we can't have that." I took my finger and began tracing where my lips had just vacated on her stomach.

"That feels good," she said, relaxing backward, staring up into the trees above us.

She started laughing.

"What?" I asked.

"Are you writing your name on my stomach?"

"Wow, you're really good. And yes, I am." I leaned over and kissed her one more time there. "I want you to remember who this stomach belongs to." I jumped to my feet and offered a hand, pulling her up.

She wrapped her arms around my neck. "So, if my stomach belongs to you, then who does yours belong to?"

"Careful now," I warned. "You're getting me all excited talking about body parts like this. Maybe we should save this discussion for our next make out session."

I rested my forehead on hers.

"*I'm* getting *you* all excited. Sure I am."

I chuckled. "You have no idea. I'm trying to be a good kid here, and you keep pushing me to my limits."

She snorted and shoved away. "You're a dork."

"Yep," I replied, grabbing her back and kissed her again while I walked forward, until she was pressed against the side of my truck.

We broke apart and watched each other for several seconds.

She bit her lip and looked away for a moment.

"What?" I asked.

"Nothing."

"Tell me."

"No."

"So there is something," I goaded, and she exhaled in exasperation.

"I was just going to say . . . I like you."

"I already knew that." I smirked, but immediately noticed her crestfallen look. I dipped in next to her ear.

"No worries, Nikki. I more than like you." I quickly pecked her cheek again before she could respond, and then took her hand and dragged her away from the truck. "Come on. It's time to throw some rocks."

"Rocks?" she questioned, completely flustered.

"Yes. We're moving on to stage two of the date—skipping rocks across the water."

"Okay," she replied, drawing out the word like I was crazy, and I was beginning to think maybe I was. But it was time to cool down and keep things easy. I was determined to catch this girl and hang on to her.

"So how have your cheer practices been going?"

I bent to examine some of the stones by the water's edge, and she did the same.

"It's been all right. We have a lot of new girls trying out to fill the spots the seniors are leaving."

"That's good," I replied even though I didn't really know anything about cheerleading, but if it interested her, it interested me. "How long have you been doing it?"

"Since junior high . . . for the school teams. I cheered for the local Pop Warner Football teams before that."

"Wow. So you've been at it for a while. I bet you're awesome. I can't wait to watch you."

She laughed. "Sure you can't."

"I'm wounded you don't think I'm serious." I clasped my hand to my chest as my eyes drifted over the length of her. "Show me something right now."

"Not a chance." She smiled, and a sweet blush stole across her face.

"Why not?"

"I don't know. Just because. It's embarrassing."

"You do it in front of hundreds of people. It can't be that bad." I skipped a rock across the water and turned to look at her again.

"It's different with just you watching."

"I disagree. This is your biggest fan right here. I think that deserves a private showing, don't you?"

She turned and tossed her stone. We both laughed when it sank immediately.

"Well, I suck at this."

I scanned the ground, finding and picking up a smooth flat rock.

"Like this." I turned her so her back was against my chest. I placed the rock in her hand, and curled mine over her fingers. "Now move this way, keeping the stone level with the water. And when you toss it, give it a little flick with your wrist."

I dropped my arm away, but continued to hold her. She did as I instructed and the rock skipped once this time before sinking.

"See. You're a natural." I kissed the top of her head before moving my mouth down to feather more on her neck.

She shifted to the side slightly, giving me better access, and I traced the area with the tip of my tongue. I felt her shudder and smiled against her skin. She tried to face me, but I kept her pinned in place, so she leaned back against my shoulder.

"You taste nice," I whispered in her ear before I nipped at her earlobe.

"You're the first person who's ever said that to me," she said with a quiet laugh.

"Good," I replied, and I meant it. I wanted to be the only one saying that kind of stuff to her. She was mine. "I think we should make our relationship exclusive."

"You mean we haven't already?" She lifted her hand and rubbed it over my cheek. "I haven't seen either of us chasing after anyone else."

"I know, but I want to put it out there. You know, make it for real." I couldn't believe how quickly she'd hooked me. I never remembered feeling this way about another girl.

I loosened my hold on her so she could turn.

"I'll be your girlfriend, Chase, if it's what you really want. I mean you have slept in my bed and everything. I guess we should make it official." She bit back a grin.

I tucked a stray hair behind her ear. "I want that too. To sleep in your bed for real—with you," I added, emphasizing my meaning.

She swallowed hard and cast her gaze away nervously before looking back. "I know you do."

"I'll wait, you know. Until whenever you decide you're ready."

"I've had guys tell me that before. It's never true." She stared at me with hurt, sad eyes that were almost my undoing.

I placed my hands on either side of her face. "None of those guys were me, Nikki. I mean it. You'll control that part of our relationship. Nothing will happen between us until you're sure. And when you are, you'll have to tell me. I won't assume anything."

She nodded. "Okay." She glanced down. "What if I'm never ready?"

I grunted. "Then I guess I'll have to become a priest or something."

She laughed. "Chase the priest? I don't think that's in the realm of possibilities."

"Why? Don't I come off as the tiniest bit religious?"

"Not really," she replied, and I appreciated her honesty.

"Well, you're wrong. I know there's got to be a God somewhere, because he sent you to me—right when I needed you most."

"Oh, Chase," she whispered, moving to caress my face.

I kissed her and vowed during every second of it I

would keep my word, even as my body raged in protest over it all. It was so difficult to do. I wanted her. If I were to do what was best for us, I'd walk away from her this second and quit placing myself directly in front of the bus threatening to run me over.

I did the opposite, though. I ran my hands down her back, cupping her hips and pressing her against me as our mouths explored each other. Her fingers tousled through my hair as she tried to pull me closer, and I ravaged her, unable to get enough as the fire she caused started storming through my veins. I didn't want to stop, and she acted like she didn't either, wrapping herself around me tighter.

Groaning, I untangled myself and took a step away. I could hardly stand to look at her, seeing my desire mirrored in her eyes. All she had to do was say the words, and I'd sweep her off her feet and carry her over to the blanket.

But the words didn't come, as we both stared at each other, trying to slow our breathing.

"Nikki, I apologize for cutting our picnic short, but I think I need to take you to the house. My mom wants to meet you."

I assumed she understood what I meant when she gave a nod. "Okay. I'd like that. She sounded very nice on the phone."

I smiled. "Mixed company would be a very good thing for us right now, I think."

We loaded our things and headed back. Halfway there she slid over and placed her hand on my knee. I stopped quickly and threw the truck into park—right there in the middle of the road—and attacked her mouth again. She let a squeal of surprise, but kissed me for several long moments until I wrenched away.

"If you don't want your first time to be right here in the front seat, I suggest you slide over there and stay there." I pointed to the passenger side.

She didn't say a word but moved as I suggested, and neither of us spoke for the rest of the drive.

~Chapter Fifteen~

I grabbed the basket with the remainder of our picnic in one hand, before taking Nikki's in the other, leading her toward the house.

"Grandma?" I called when we entered.

"In here, Chase," she replied from the rear of the house. "Are you back already?"

I followed the sound of her voice into the spacious country kitchen, finding her kneading some dough in a giant stainless steel pan.

"Is Mom here? I didn't see her car outside."

"She ran to town to get a couple of things from the grocery store for dinner. She should be back soon. Hi Nikki, how are you? I'd shake your hand, but . . . ," she trailed off and glanced down at her work.

"No worries," Nikki replied. "I'm good, thank you. Your home is very lovely."

"Well, I'm glad Chase has decided to start bringing some of his friends here. It's nice to have young people around the place again."

"If you keep cooking food like you have been, I wager we'll have the whole school showing up at our door, Grandma. Thank you for the amazing lunch." I set the basket on the counter and gave her a kiss on the cheek.

"It was delicious," Nikki added.

"Did you eat it all?" Grandma asked with a smile.

"Heck, no. You packed enough in here to feed an army." I reached inside and started pulling out the leftover containers, and Nikki helped me put them in the fridge.

"We need to get you eating more. It'll be good for you to pack some pounds on for football. I imagine Grandpa will want to beef up your foods now that early weight training is starting."

"I'm okay with eating more. Just leave me thin enough so I can attempt to waddle down the field at a reasonable pace, at least." I turned to Nikki. "Will you still like me if I'm fat?"

Nikki laughed. "I can't imagine you that way. I don't really see it being an issue for you with all your good genes."

I looked down and rubbed my hands over my pants. "I do have good jeans, don't I? This pair is one of my favorites."

"You're a dork." She grinned and elbowed me in the ribs.

"You're saying you're into dorks then?"

She giggled. "I guess so." She turned to my grandma. "Is there anything we can help you with, Mrs. Johnson?"

"No, sweetheart. Thank you for asking. Why don't you have Chase take you to see the animals while you're waiting for his mom to get home?"

"That's a good idea." I took Nikki's hand again. "I'll introduce you to the horse I learned to ride on."

We went out the door and made our way across the lawn in the direction of the barn.

"I like it here," Nikki said, as she gazed around. "It's so peaceful."

There was only the low hum of a tractor in the distance, and I could see the dust churning up behind Grandpa as he plowed one of the far fields to ready it for planting.

"It is nice. I didn't think I would like it when I first

moved here, but it sort of grew on me."

We entered the barn, and I took her to where Mitzi was standing in her stall. The horse neighed softly and pushed her nose into my palm, nuzzling.

"This is Mitzi," I said, reaching for a carrot from the bucket where grandpa kept his stash of treats.

"She's beautiful." Nikki stroked the mare down the white star on her nose. "So tall too."

"This horse is an old gal, but that's what makes her the best in my opinion. She's got all that life she's lived behind her—a wise lady now."

"What a nice thing to say." Nikki smiled. "If only everyone saw things that way."

We stood together in silence, petting and feeding the animal. I slipped my arm around Nikki's waist and watched her. She was so pretty.

"Hey, come here. I want to show you something else." I led her to the hayloft ladder. "You have to see the view from up there."

I sent her up first and followed after her, before going to the door and sliding it open.

"Oh, this is wonderful," she exclaimed, looking out at the far reaches of the land.

"I could sit here all day and stare at it."

She stepped nearer to the edge.

"Watch out!" I exclaimed, grabbing her and spinning her away, toppling us both into the giant mound of straw behind us.

She landed with an "oomph" on top of me and slugged me in the shoulder.

"You scared me to death, Chase Walker!"

"Better scared than dead." I laughed, enclosing my arms around her tighter.

"I wasn't even close and you know it! You wanted an excuse to throw me in the hay."

"That's right. And it worked, didn't it?" I glanced

over her face. "I could let you go—if you really want me to."

She stared at me, her hair dropping to caress the edges of her features. "Don't let go." She closed the distance and pressed her lips to mine.

I sighed and gave in to the emotions coursing through me. I was tired of fighting my attraction. I wanted to wrap myself up in her and forget about everything else. I rolled over so she was underneath me and brushed my fingers through her silky hair, tangling it with the straw beneath it. I kissed her passionately, running my tongue into her mouth, and she let out a tiny moan as she ran her hands up and down my back.

The niggling voice in my subconscious mind reminded me of my vow to take things slowly. I pushed it away, not wanting to listen. I wanted to lose it with her. However, I couldn't ignore it, because it kept getting louder the longer we kissed.

Sliding my hand down her arm, I pulled it away, pinning it above her head, then did the same with the other. I held her there while I kissed a trail over her cheek, down her neck to her collarbone.

She arched, struggling against where I had her restrained. "I want to touch you too," she whispered.

"I know you do," I breathed out in a ragged voice. She had no idea what she was doing with those touches—not that having her squirming against me was helping things much either.

"Chase, are you in here?" My mom's voice floated up to the hayloft, and I dropped my head briefly to Nikki's chest before I slid off to lie next to her.

"We're up here, Mom," I replied, turning to look at Nikki who was quickly trying to pick the straw out of her hair. "Leave it. It looks good on you." I chuckled. "Embrace it."

She flopped back down with an exasperated sigh as

my mom popped her head over the railing.

"Oh, I'm not interrupting anything, am I?" she asked, glancing between the two of us.

"No." I gestured to the straw. "Come join us. I brought Nikki up here to show her the view.

"The view . . . is that what they're calling it these days?" Mom smiled at both of us as she settled in beside me. She leaned over and extended her hand to Nikki. "Hi. I'm Tori. It's a pleasure to meet you."

Nikki sat up slightly and grasped her hand. Her face flushed a bit in embarrassment. "It's nice to meet you too. Chase always speaks so highly of you."

My mom smiled wider and looked at me. "Does he now?" She released Nikki and gently squeezed me on the leg. "That's nice to know. I have to say he does the same about you too. I'd imagine it has something to do with why he brought you up here to show you the view as well."

I choked a little before laughing. Nikki reddened more.

"Don't be embarrassed, Nikki. I told Chase how much I used to admire this place with his father too."

"And there goes the mood," I groaned. "Please spare us any further details, Mom." Imagining my parents making out was not on my list of fun things to do.

Nikki elbowed me. "I think it's romantic." She giggled. "I wonder if your grandparents have kissed up here as well."

"Oh, you can count on that," my mom quickly replied, and I protested even louder.

"Mom, you have successfully ruined this hayloft for me for the rest of forever. I'm never going to be able to sit up here now."

"Just think of it as love spanning the generations, son. This loft is part of your heritage."

I snorted. "If you say so."

"I do. Your dad and I spent many days dreaming and making plans for our future while we stared at the view. Your grandpa would take you off to learn to ride the horses so we could have a little alone time. It was nice. We made some good decisions together up here." She gave a heavy, tired sigh and picked up a piece of straw, twirling it between her fingers.

"I'm sorry he's gone," I said quietly. "I know you miss him."

She nodded. "I do. But he would want us to get on with our lives and be happy. I think we're both finally trying to do that now."

It was quiet for a few moments before she spoke again. "Chase tells me you lost your father also, Nikki."

"Yeah. He had cancer, though, so we had a little more time to prepare ourselves for what we knew was coming. I was happy he wasn't suffering anymore after he passed, but it was still really hard on all of us."

"I can imagine," Mom replied. "How's your family holding up?"

"We're doing okay. My mom has a decent job so we get by all right. The younger kids don't remember my dad much though, so she's always showing them pictures and telling them stories to keep him alive in their minds. She's had other guys ask her on dates and stuff, but she always turns them down. I wish she wouldn't. I'd like her to find some of her own happiness again."

"Well, if there's one thing I've learned, it's that each of us grieves in our own way. There's no right way to do it, you just do. I imagine when she's ready to take that step and move on, she will. It sounds like she's content just being with her kids right now. There's nothing wrong with that either."

A silence fell over the three of us as we stared out

over the gently sloping valley and low-lying hills beyond.

"Thanks for being there for my boy." My mom turned to Nikki. "He's needed a good friend like you."

Nikki smiled. "It's my pleasure, but really you should thank him for being my friend. He was quite . . . persistent."

I laughed again and leaned over to peck her on the cheek. "What she actually means, Mom, is I drove her to insanity getting her to go out with me."

My mom chuckled. "That's Chase for you. I've never known him to back down from something he's really wanted. He's like a pit bull. He'll keep attacking until he gets it the way he wants it."

"Great. Now I'm being compared to a dog. You so aren't helping my image." I rolled my eyes at her.

"It's good to be determined. It will get you far in life."

"What do you want to do after you graduate?" Nikki asked me.

I shrugged. "I'm not sure what vocation I want to go into yet, but I would love to play football for as long as I can. I was hoping I could get a college scholarship or something, but I don't know if quitting part way through last year's season will affect my stats too much."

"I don't think it will," Mom interjected. "If you keep playing as well as you have been or better, I don't see how they could pass by you. I'm sure they can take personal hardship into consideration too."

"Maybe. We'll see."

"So you don't have anything else you'd like to do?" Nikki continued in her search for more insight.

"Well, my dad was a businessman, but I don't know if I'm cut out for an office job. Other than playing video games, I like weight lifting and sports, so maybe something with athletic training or physical therapy would be good."

"What about you, Nikki?" my mom asked.

"I want to be a counselor. My dad knew a therapist from his job at the hospital, and my mom helped me get an internship with her. She does the drug abuse classes. I'd really like to work with people and assist them through the hard times if I could. Maggie's great to work for, isn't she, Chase?"

I nodded. "I've never sat in on the group, but she seems like a very nice lady. She's always been fair with me."

"And suddenly the reason you rush off to community service every Saturday has just become clearer," my mom said wryly.

"He never told you we worked together?"

She shook her head. "No. And here I was being so proud he was taking things seriously."

"I am taking things seriously," I said, piping up to defend myself. "Everything about Nikki is serious to me."

The two of them burst out laughing.

"Come on," my mom said, patting my leg before she stood. "Let's go see if your grandma needs any help with supper preparations. It's still a few hours away, but she's been making bread all day. I don't want to wear her out. Are you staying for dinner tonight, Nikki?"

Nikki glanced at me in question.

"You don't have to ask me. I'd keep you here twenty-four/seven if I had any say in the matter."

She blushed again. "Yes, I'll stay, I guess."

"Good," my mom replied. "It'll be nice to have a pretty girl at the table. Now I suggest you put this boy to work picking all that straw out of your hair before you come inside." She turned and looked pointedly at me. "Don't mess her up anymore, mister."

I grinned. "You parents. Always taking the fun out of everything."

"I mean it," she added, stabbing her finger in my direction.

"Yes, ma'am." I sighed and sat up to scoot behind Nikki. I began to dutifully do as she said. I waited for my mom to disappear over the railing before I spoke again. "I, personally, think you look great with all of this sticking out all over your head."

"I heard that," Mom's voice floated back to us, and we laughed.

"I like your mom." Nikki said with a smile.

"That's good, because I can tell she likes you as well." I brushed her pokey hair away from her neck and leaned into kiss her there. "And that works great for me, because I like you too."

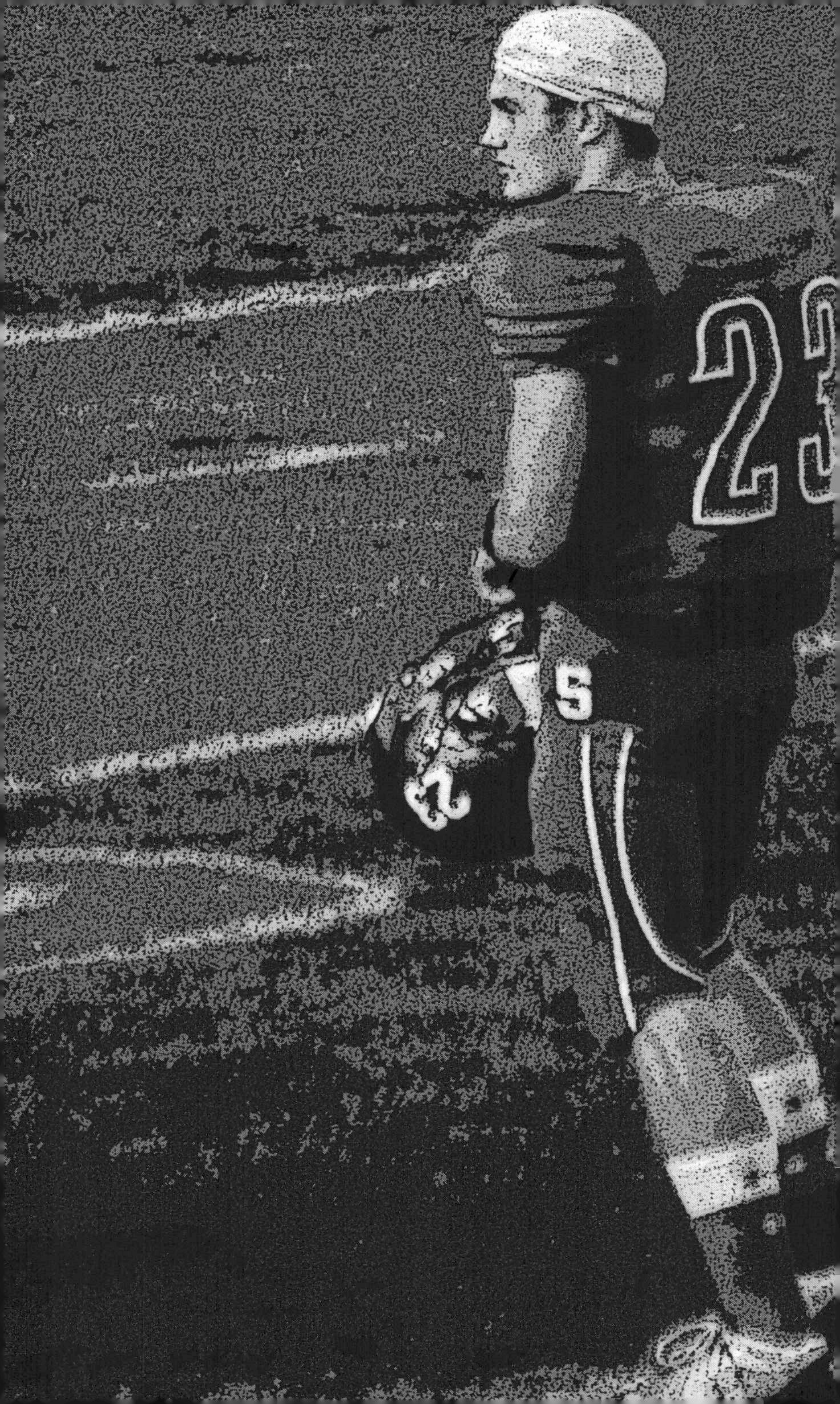
23

~Chapter Sixteen~

I had to stop myself from chuckling at the group of girls scattered across the gym floor facing the rest of the student body. I couldn't remotely imagine how scary it must be to have a tryout in front of the entire school. There were definitely lots of kids who weren't taking it seriously, and a handful were shouting catcalls to the participants.

I didn't really care, though, because I only had eyes for Nikki. She was dressed in a fitted white tee shirt and blue shorts which showed off her pretty curves and very shapely legs. I was positive I wasn't the only guy watching her, and I wished I could pull the fire alarm so no one else had the pleasure of staring while she bounced around out there.

The girls were rotating in sections, so each row had the chance to stand in the very front and be seen and judged. I waited for Nikki's to come forward and do their cheer. Reaching between my knees, I grabbed the giant white poster I'd made, with the number ten written in big bold letters and held it up.

Nikki noticed immediately and flushed a bright red. I chuckled, enjoying myself completely. Several students began looking and pointing at me, laughing. I didn't care. Every time Nikki came forward, I flashed my sign, signaling my opinion clearly to the adult judging panel as well.

Tryouts lasted about thirty minutes, and at the end

we had to check off a sheet of paper with our favorite picks for the squad. I put three checks next to Nikki's name and a couple next to her friends, Tana and Brittney too. They were both really good.

We were released a little early for lunch, so I went out to my truck to wait for Nikki. I left the door open and turned the stereo on loudly while I watched people piling into cars and leaving. It wasn't long before I saw her hurrying across the lot to join me, and I jumped out of the truck to meet her.

"You were great, baby." I smiled, pulling her against me.

"Really? I was actually kind of flustered because you kept flashing that dang sign." She wrapped her arms around me, hugging tightly, and I laughed.

"Sorry. I didn't think about that. I just wanted to make sure everyone there knew you were the best."

"Whatever, but, hey, I'm glad *you* thought so." She popped up on her tiptoes to give me a kiss on the cheek. "Are you ready to eat?"

"In a minute. Brett's coming with us today, but he had to turn in a late assignment before he left so he wouldn't get detention."

"I wish I'd have known. I would've invited Tana to go with us too."

"Tana? Why?"

Nikki smiled. "You boys are so blind sometimes. She's had a crush on him for ages."

I mulled over this new information. "That's interesting."

"How come?"

"Because I've been trying to get Brett to go out with her so we could double date. He said she dumped him in sixth grade. I got the impression the two were way through with each other."

Nikki shook her head. "Not Tana. She's always liked

him."

"Why'd she break up with him then?"

"Her parents made her. They said she was too young to have a boyfriend."

"Ah, I see." I brushed some of her hair back from her face and kissed her lightly. "Here he comes now. Maybe we should play matchmaker for them. What do you think?"

She smiled widely and kissed me back. "I think that sounds fabulous."

By the time early weight training rolled around after school, I'd convinced Brett to ask Tana out. He seemed skeptical she still liked him, but I told him Nikki was positive. We'd set up a double date to the movie for the weekend to help take the awkwardness of the first date off them.

The guys from the team were all gathering around the weight stands picking what they needed for the different equipment we were working on. Machines were clanking loudly by the time Coach Hardin walked in and blew his whistle to get our attention.

"Welcome, boys. I'm happy to see so many of you here. I know we'll get several more when the official practices start this summer, but I think this will help all of you gain an edge. I realize many of you are returning this year, but we have some new people here as well." He looked pointedly at me before moving on. "I'm excited to see what some of you have to offer. We have several positions which have been vacated by the graduating seniors. We'll be filling and shifting things around until we move like a well-oiled machine. Just because you played somewhere this year, doesn't mean you'll have that spot next year. The best man will get the starter positions, and you will be placed where we feel you'll best serve the team. So until things are decided, work hard and run fast."

"Thanks, Coach," someone said from the back of the room. The rest of us added our agreements and returned to what we'd been doing.

Toward the end of the session, the coach blew his whistle again. "That's good for today. I'd like to see the following guys before you leave today—Chad Thompson, Wes Miller, Brett Dodson, and Chase Walker."

I shot my eyebrows up in surprise as I glanced over at Brett in question.

He shrugged. "I don't know, but if I had to wager a guess, I'd say Coach is planning on taking you for a test run. Chad and Wes are running backs, and I'm the center."

Great, I thought. *An impromptu try out for quarterback.*

I hadn't been prepared for this, and I tried to calm my sudden flutter of nerves, reminding myself football was like breathing to me . . . second nature.

After all the others had filtered from the room, my grandpa stepped through the door.

"Warren, glad you could make it," Coach Hardin said, extending his hand.

"Wouldn't miss it." Grandpa sent a smile and a friendly wink my way.

Coach Hardin turned to address those of us who remained. "Boys, I'd like to take you down to the field and have you run a few snaps and passing drills with Chase. We're looking at him as a possible quarterback based on what Warren has told us about him, and some of his past statistics. I know it's early for this, but we want to know what all of our options are this year. Is that okay with each of you?"

"Sure thing, Coach," Brett replied. "I've been anxious to see if my buddy here is for real, or all talk."

He punched me playfully on the shoulder.

"Hey! Be careful. That's my throwing arm." I gave a fake wince as I rubbed it. "You probably killed my whole tryout now."

Brett laughed and rolled his eyes. "Whatever dude. I didn't hit you that hard."

"You kids go on down to the field lockers, grab several footballs, and start warming up. Warren and I will join you in a couple of minutes."

The four of us took off, and I dug my cell from my pocket to message Nikki.

Grandpa's here. Coach wants 2 try me out with some field drills 2day. Text when I'm done. Probably won't get 2 C U 2night.

She replied right away. K. No worries. Good luck.

Thx, I wrote back. Luv U.

I hit send before I realized what I'd done.

Damn, damn, damn. I told my girlfriend I loved her for the first time in a text. I hadn't even meant to. It had seemed like the natural thing to say.

My phone buzzed loudly in my hands, and I stared at the reply.

Ummm . . . U luv me?

"Chase? You gonna stand in the middle of the street all day, or are you gonna come do this?" Chad's voice called, and I looked up to see the others way ahead.

"I'm coming." I hurried to catch up as I sent a reply.

Sorry. Busy. Call U as soon as I'm able. I hit send and turned my phone off, feeling bad for leaving her hanging. I hoped to high heaven I'd be able to concentrate on what I needed to do now.

"Who were you talking to?" Brett asked.

"Nikki. Just telling her I'd be late tonight."

"Man, she's got you on the ol' ball and chain already, doesn't she?" Wes hooted. "You sound like some old married guy."

I laughed it off with a shrug. "Fine by me. I'm sure there could be a lot worse things in the world than being married to someone like Nikki."

Chad groaned. "Dude. You got it bad, bro."

"She's great girl," I said a bit defensively.

"Back it down, Chase." Brett said, giving me an elbow. "We're just razzing you a bit. We think it's cool the two of you hooked up. Don't we guys?"

"Sure. She's a hot chick."

That only inflamed me more. I left and went out onto the field. Once I hit the center, I dropped all the balls I was carrying and flexed and stretched my arm.

Brett picked one up. "You ready?"

"Yep. Fire away."

Brett moved away a few yards and tossed me the ball. I caught it and threw it back—gradually increasing the distance between us until I was warm.

"Nice steady pitches there, Chase," Coach Hardin said as he and my grandpa arrived. "Let's see how you do with a moving target, shall we? Brett, come hike for us."

The three boys lined up, and I took my place behind Brett several feet and called the snap. I caught it easily and watched as Chad and Wes took off running different routes.

"To Wes," Coach called, and I bombed it the long distance down the field.

Wes turned with perfect timing and caught the ball easily.

"Good job. Run it again."

We set up once more, but this time coach directed me to throw to Chad who was farther downfield. I was completely locked in, easily judging the speed of my future teammate, and I threw the ball.

Chad reached out and caught it, turning to run toward the end zone.

Coach blew the whistle. "Do you feel comfortable enough to try out receiving too?" he asked.

I nodded.

"Okay. Let's try that now."

This time Wes took the snap, and I ran the route. He threw his pass, which was slightly wobbly, but accurate. It was a little high, but I was able to jump up and catch it.

"Do it again, but this time, Chad you defend, and try to cause pass interference."

We took off once more, and Chad ran good defense, managing to tip the pass as it came, causing the ball to change course. I had to dive across the grass to get it, but still managed to do so before it hit the ground.

Coach called us back again. "Great grab, Chase. Now I want you to quarterback again and throw to Wes. Chad I want you to play defense and try to get him. Brett you're the lineman defending your quarterback."

Brett hiked the ball, and I rolled back. Chad clashed with him while he tried breaking by to get to me. I waited for Wes to hit his position and threw the ball right before Chad reached me, wrapping me up and swinging me around.

The ball hit Wes perfectly, and he turned to run toward the end zone.

Coach blew his whistle again and brought us together. "Thanks for helping me out boys. I think I've seen enough for today. Gather these things up and put them away. Then you can take off."

"That was a blast," Brett said as we picked up the scattered footballs. "I can't wait for the season to start again."

I felt the same excitement coursing through me. I'd loved playing football from the time I was in peewee leagues as a kid. I liked to play all sports, but football was my thing. I hadn't realized how much I'd missed it lately.

My thoughts drifted to images of my dad standing on all those sidelines cheering for me, and I felt a heaviness settle over my heart.

"You okay? You seem kind of sad for a guy who just impressed the head coach." Brett studied me with a worried look.

"I'm alright," I said with a sigh. "I was thinking it's gonna be weird not having my dad here with me this year. He used to help coach my teams as a volunteer. I'm used to seeing him there, giving me instructions and pep talks when I needed it."

Brett didn't say anything for a moment, casting his gaze around the field before speaking. "That guy will be on the sidelines for you now, if you let him." He pointed to my grandpa. "He's done nothing but sing your praises. I'll be there with you too, and so will Nikki. I know we won't take the spot of your dad, but you have friends if you want them." He shuffled some of the balls he was carrying and clapped me on the shoulder before he continued on toward the field house.

I stood there staring after him, letting his words sink in. He was right. No one could replace my dad, but there were others waiting in the wings for me, if I'd let them in. I didn't have to be alone if I didn't want to be. I'd withdrawn from everyone to nurse my hurts by myself. Nikki had shown me it didn't have to be that way. Could I start trusting other people too?

"Brett. Wait up." I hurried to catch up. "Wanna come to dinner at my house tonight? Grandma's making steak and potatoes."

"Steak?" Chad's head popped up. "Am I invited?"

"Sure." I grinned. "You can all come. Just let me ask my grandma and make sure it's okay with her. If not, we'll go pick up some burgers for everyone on the way."

I called home, and she actually sounded excited to

have the guys over, insisting there was plenty for everyone. I thanked her for the impromptu dinner party and hung up.

"She says come on over."

"Sweet. Let me call my mom," Wes said, digging out his phone.

"Okay. I'll go tell my grandpa what the plan is."

I left the locker room and headed to where he was still visiting with Coach Hardin on the field.

"Good job today, Chase," Coach said as I approached. "I'm very excited to have you on the team. I think you'll be a great addition."

"Thanks for giving me the opportunity to try out as your quarterback too. I'll do my best wherever you want to put me, though. I just want to play."

Coach looked me over for a second before he turned to my grandpa. "Great kid you got here, Warren. Thanks again for coming out." He patted me on the shoulder as he walked past. "See you tomorrow."

"Goodnight, Jeff," Grandpa said before glancing at me, a grin spreading across his face. "He's impressed. You did well."

I shrugged as if it were no big deal. "It was fun. Made me excited for the season."

"Me too." Grandpa chuckled. "I enjoy working with these boys. They're a good group."

"Well, I really like everyone I've met so far."

Except for Jeremy Winters, I added mentally, but there was no point in bringing that up right now, since he wasn't going to be here anymore.

"I'm glad you're starting to make some good friends."

"Speaking of that, I called Grandma, and she said it was okay with her if I brought these guys over for dinner tonight. Is that cool with you?"

Grandpa chuckled. "Yeah, it's cool with me. Let's go

home."

"I'll meet you there shortly—there's one little pit stop I need to make on the way."

"Let me guess . . . Nikki's house?"

I nodded. "I'll only be a minute, but I need to talk to her about something."

"Well, hurry up. You don't want to keep your guests waiting."

"I will. Thanks, Grandpa." I ran off the field, pausing to tell the guys to go on ahead and follow Grandpa home, I'd be there as soon as possible.

~Chapter Seventeen~

I sent a text to Nikki telling her I was on my way over, and she was outside waiting for me on the porch swing when I pulled up. I released a big sigh, not exactly sure how to approach this subject with her. Honestly, I was feeling foolish. I'd never told any girl I loved her before, and while I was sure that's what I was experiencing, it just seemed so sudden.

I climbed out of the truck and shoved my hands in my pockets as I walked up the sidewalk. Her pleasant expression didn't change as I approached, and she moved to the right to make room. Shaking my head, I chose to lean against the railing across from her. She looked disappointed with my decision.

"How was practice?" she asked, breaking the awkward silence between us.

"It was good, I guess. Grandpa seems to think the coach liked what he saw." I studied the toes of my shoes.

"You can sit by me, you know." She patted the bench.

I denied her again. "I'm all sweaty."

"I don't mind." She smiled, but it fell from her face when I didn't move.

"Did you hear if you made the cheer squad yet?" I tried warming up with small talk.

She nodded and looked away.

"Well, are you gonna tell me what they said?" I chuckled.

"Are you mad at me?" she asked.

"What? No! Why would you think that?"

"You seem so . . . aloof."

I dragged a hand through my hair. "I don't mean to be. I'm . . . I'm nervous, I guess."

"Because of the text?"

"Yes." I was determined to muddle through this. "I've never told a girl I loved her before, and this time it was a complete accident. It slipped out, and I pressed send before I realized what I'd written. That's what happens when you text while distracted, apparently."

"Oh, I see." She looked positively crestfallen.

"What do you see?"

"That you didn't mean to say it."

I sat next to her, but she wouldn't look at me, so I lifted her chin until she had to glance at me. "No, I didn't mean to say it you in that way—not that it wasn't true."

It took a few seconds for the meaning of my words to sink in, and then her mouth opened slightly.

"Oh," she said softly. "Wait. What are you saying exactly?"

I laughed. "I'm saying I love you, Nikki. You have no idea how much you mean to me. You don't have to reply, but I want you to know my feelings for you are real. You've been the greatest gift in my life—the girl I never knew I always wanted."

She leaned toward me and brushed her lips lightly against mine before tracing the outline of my mouth. "Thank you, Chase. I love you too."

"You're not just saying it because I did, are you?" I couldn't look away from her beautiful face.

"No. I mean it. But I don't know if I would've ever had the courage to tell you first."

"Well, that doesn't matter anymore now, does it?" I slipped my arm around her waist and brought her closer, kissing her harder this time.

She slid her hands up to my cheeks, holding me there as our tongues danced together.

I groaned and moved away. "I wish I could stay longer, but I've got to go. All the guys are at my house waiting to have dinner."

"And you came here first? Why? We could've waited to talk."

I grinned. "I wasn't about to leave you hanging. Besides you're my first priority."

"Really? I like that." She stood and pulled me up.

"Why do you still sound surprised? I just told you I love you. Isn't that the way it's supposed to be between two people in love?"

"I'm not used to it yet." She seemed a little shy, staring at my chest as she drew with her finger there. "Say it to me again."

I leaned in until my lips were brushing against her earlobe. "I love you, Nikki Wagner," I whispered. "I love you, and I want you in ways you could never imagine."

"Oh, I can imagine plenty." Her breathing was shallow and rapid.

I kissed her neck. "Unfortunately, I'm going to have to leave the exploring of that statement to a later date."

"Yeah, you should go." She swallowed hard and tipped her head back even more.

I mumbled an agreement as my lips slid farther across her skin. She felt so silky and smooth, and she smelled so good.

"Chase," she said softly, sinking her fingertips into my hair.

"Yes?" I licked her with the tip of my tongue.

I felt her tremble. "You need to go."

"I know." I closed my mouth over her flesh and sucked lightly.

She jumped a little. "You're going to give me a

hickey if you don't stop."

"I don't care." I'd love to see my mark on her, but I leaned away instead, seeing both desire and sorrow written on her features.

"What's wrong?" I asked, afraid to touch her again for fear I'd be captured back into her web.

"I wish you didn't have to go."

I chuckled. "Me either. I'm sorry."

"Don't be. I'm so glad you're having the guys over for the evening. It'll be fun."

When I didn't move, she steered me toward the steps.

"Leave," she ordered.

"Yes, ma'am."

"And call me before you go to bed."

"Yes, ma'am," I replied again as she pushed me down the stairs to the sidewalk.

"Have a good night. I love you."

I growled, reaching up to yank her to me. She fell against me with a laugh, and I kissed her one last time before I set her aside and spanked her on the rump.

"Quit detaining me." I grinned.

"Whatever. Leave." She giggled.

"You first. Go inside."

She sighed as if she were totally put out. "Goodnight, Chase," she called over her shoulder before she slipped into the house.

"Goodnight, my pretty girl," I whispered even though I knew she couldn't hear me. I turned and jogged over to my truck.

"Sorry I took so long," I apologized when I walked inside. "It took slightly longer than I anticipated." I glanced at the three boys who were playing my video game console.

"Yeah, it's hard to rush when you have your tongue

stuck down a girl's throat." Wes snickered.

"Jealous much?" I stabbed back.

"Kind of," he replied.

"You're not late either. The three of us ran home and showered real quick first," Brett informed me.

"Okay, good."

"Your grandma sent us up here. She said she'd holler when dinner was ready."

"Awesome. Well, then I'll go get cleaned up too."

"Better hurry, dude. If your grandma calls while you're in there, I'm not promising we'll save you any. It smells like heaven down there."

I chuckled. "Wait until you taste it."

I left them to their game and made my way to my room, dropping my things in a pile on the floor and going to the drawer to grab some items. My attention was caught by Turk who was swimming at the edge of his bowl, facing me. I'd deluded myself into thinking this fish was my friend, loving how he always swam to the edge when I entered.

"Hey, big guy. How was your day?" I tapped lightly on the glass before I grabbed his food and dropped a few flakes in for him. "Mine was pretty good, I guess. I told Nikki I loved her today . . . in a text message." I scrutinized him for his reaction, but he didn't move. "I can see you're dumbfounded. I was too for a while. I've got company now, though, so I'll fill you in on all the details later. Enjoy your supper."

The guys were missing when I returned, and I knew that could only mean one thing—dinner was on the table. I found everyone in the kitchen passing around the food and dishing it out.

"You're right on time, Chase," my mom said as she glanced over to smile at our unexpected guest.

Greg. Yay. My appetite suddenly seemed a little on

the iffy side.

I pulled out the only available chair—next to him of course—and started piling food onto my plate.

"So your grandpa tells me you really wowed the coach today. Good job. We need someone to try and fill those shoes Jeremy Winters is leaving behind," Greg spoke, and I felt the heat creep up under my collar.

I didn't miss the furtive looks that passed between the other guys.

"He's better than Jeremy," Brett said as he lifted a piece of steak to his mouth, and I never wanted to hug a guy so much before.

"I agree," Chad added. "His throws are a lot straighter and much easier to catch."

"Don't judge until we try it under pressure." I took a bite of mashed potatoes.

"Probably a good idea," Grandpa agreed. "Don't count your chickens before they've hatched. That being said though, Chase did put on a good show. I'm anxious to see how things will go this season."

"I'm assuming you'll still be helping as the team trainer this season?" Greg directed the comment to my grandpa.

"Yes. I like putting my old corpsman training to use and taping up those injuries and stuff. Got to keep these boys healthy somehow."

"Well, I think it's great you've volunteered to do that all these years. I miss playing football, and I'd love to coach, but unfortunately my schedule doesn't always allow that. I'm in the seats every Friday, though, ready to cheer them on." He looked at me with a grin. "It'll be nice to have someone in particular to yell for."

I tried not to groan. Talk about overkill. My mom was practically glowing over his statements, and she reached over to pat his arm. I swear it was as if he'd said he discovered the cure for cancer or something.

"Thanks," I mumbled, when she turned and threw me the stink eye for being rude and not responding. I tuned out most of the rest of the dinner conversation, contributing only when absolutely necessary.

When I was done eating, I cleared my place and went outside. I opened my truck and dug around beneath the driver's seat until I found what I was searching for—my old football. I hadn't touched it since the day my dad died, leaving it shoved under there since I knew we'd never throw together again. I pulled it out, almost reverently, rolling it in my hands as I gripped it.

"There you are," Brett's voice came from the porch. "He's here guys."

I shut the door and leaned against the truck as they came to join me.

"Everything okay?" Wes asked.

"Yeah. Just digging out my old ball. I thought we could toss it around together."

"Sure," he replied. "I have one in my truck too. Let me go get it."

They followed me as I walked into the area between the house and the barn where the light from the two places was better. Brett stood by me, and Chad and Wes lined up across from us. We began throwing, naturally drifting farther and farther apart as much as the space would let us. I was totally lost in the ease of the repetitive motion when I caught movement out of the corner of my eye and turned to look.

Greg and my mom were standing next to his vehicle, and he had his arms wrapped around her waist. He was whispering something in her ear and she was giggling.

The football hit me square in the chest, knocking the air from my lungs with a whoosh and falling to the ground.

Chad started laughing as I bent to retrieve it.

"You're supposed to catch it," he hollered.

I picked the ball up and walked toward him, suddenly out of the mood to throw anymore. I gestured toward the barn with a slight jerk of my head, and they joined me inside.

"You don't like Greg much, do you?" Wes asked, not missing a thing.

I shrugged. "I'm sure he's a great guy, but I'm not too thrilled with him sniffing around my mom."

"Take it easy on him," Brett said. "He's been through a lot of heartache too. They're probably really good for each other."

"I don't want to think about it." I sounded sharper than I'd intended, and a silence followed. "Hey, I'm sorry. I don't mean to be such a pain. It's just a lot to deal with."

"I can help you with that." Chad pulled a small baggie out of his pocket and dangled it. "Want something to take the edge off?"

I stared at the blunt, wishing I could take it—wanting to take it. I could feel Brett's gaze drilling a hole into me as he waited to see what I would do. "I can't. Thanks for the offer, though."

He put the bag away. "Whatever. You know where to find me if you change your mind."

"Still trying to stick to your grandpa's rules?" Brett asked.

I nodded. "It makes life a little easier. Plus Nikki worries about me. She works for a substance abuse therapist." I chuckled wryly. "That's where I do my community service hours."

Chad groaned. "That sucks. You sound like one of those infomercials, "I'm not only the president, I'm a client too."

I rolled my eyes. "You're a dork."

"Yes, I am. But I'm a dork who can get high."

"And sell too, apparently. You're crazy to do that. If you get caught, you're gonna kill your college scholarship chances."

"Guess I better not get caught then," he replied, giving me a warning glance.

I laughed. "You don't have to worry about me. I'm on your side. Consider me the poster child for substance abuse."

"Good. Glad we're cool."

I shook my head. "It's your life. Who am I to tell you how to live it?"

If only I were so lucky.

Part Two

~Chapter Eighteen~

Brett snapped the ball, and I fell back into the pocket while I looked for a receiver. I found Chad as my line held the opposing team away and powered the ball through the air toward him. It was a perfect throw, dead on. He caught it easily, before turning to run the next thirty yards for a touchdown. The referee threw his arms into the air to signal the score, and I slapped the helmets of my lineman as I ran off the grass so the field goal team could come on.

"And number twenty-three, quarterback, Chase Walker, connects on another long pass to number eighty-two, Chad Thompson, bringing the score to Timberwolves twenty, Mountain Lions, seven!"

The crowd was going wild, eager to rub the play in the face of the opposing fans, one of our big rivals from Cooley.

"Great job, Chase," Coach Hardin said, punching my shoulder pads as I came off.

"Thanks." I removed my headgear and headed over to the water cooler on a folding table. I couldn't help the quick glance to where my girl was currently being tossed into the air by the rest of the cheer squad in the middle of a routine.

She was amazing. I had to give her that.

Get your head in the game, Chase, I growled internally and returned my attention to the field.

The extra point was good, and the kickoff team headed onto the field. I looked at the scoreboard. Three minutes left. This game was in the bag. We just needed the defense to hold them or force a turn over.

"Put me in, Coach. I can play defense too."

"You've done your part, Chase. Let these guys have a chance at it. If I need you to go in, I'll send you. Take a rest for a minute." He looked away and began talking to one of the other coaches.

I watched the defense line up against the Mountain Lions, and they snapped the ball. One of our guys barreled through the opposition and sacked their quarterback.

"Yeah!" I yelled, pumping my fist into the air. I swaggered down the sideline, slapping the back of my teammates helmets, as the crowd roared in the stands. I knew this was going to be a huge win for us. Even though we were undefeated for the season, the first three games had been non-conference games against less-than-challenging teams. Going into conference with a win straight off the bat, and against Cooley too, was going to send our message to every other team out there. We were in it to win it.

"Pass!" The guys on the sideline started yelling as Cooley set up to throw long and make up for their lost yards during the last play. Their quarterback threw the ball, and we all watched with baited breath, the crowd jumping to its feet as number sixty-four, Jace Davidson, vaulted himself into the air and intercepted the ball, turning to run toward our goal line.

The whole team shifted as we ran down the sidelines cheering him on. "Go, go, go!" I shouted, joining the others, and he made it a good twenty yards before he was tackled.

"Chase! Offense! You're up!" Coach hollered. "You boys have got this game. Let's wrap it up good now."

I was well aware of the time on the board. Two and a half minutes left. I was going to take my time calling the snaps, control the ball, and run the clock down. We needed to go twenty-five yards for a touchdown. We could do this.

Coach called the play, and I knew I was passing up the middle to Wes this time. I took the snap and stepped back as I looked for my man. One of Cooley's players broke through the line, headed right for me. I held my ground, waiting for an opportunity to throw the ball. He was getting closer, though, and I knew he was going to hit me.

There was a sudden blur as my teammate, Glen Jackson, bulldozed past me and took the guy down with a hard thud before he could touch me. I saw Wes break away from his defender and turn. I threw the ball straight for him.

He caught it easily, but was tackled immediately on the five-yard line. The ball was called down, and I turned to give Glen a hand up.

"Great coverage, man." I gave him a high five as we moved with the rest of team to set up again.

"Nice pass," he replied, with a grin. "I'm having fun. Let's finish this."

I glanced over to the coach and watched for his next call. He shouted out the numbers. We were going to run this one right up the middle. We got in position, and I waited for the clock to click down a few seconds more. I called the snap and faked the handoff to Chad. He folded his arms as if he were protecting the ball and took off. The line shifted, opening a hole right up the middle, and I took off, heading straight into the end zone.

"Chase Walker for six!" the announcer's voice came loudly over the speakers as the fans rose and cheered.

Chad ran over and the two of us jumped up for a celebratory chest bump against each other's shoulder pads.

"Nice fake," I said, as we ran off the field together.

"This game is ours." He smiled widely.

"Yes, it is."

We were greeted with a bunch of high fives as we took our places on the sidelines and watched the kicking team easily score.

"The extra point is good, fans! Let's hear it for our Silver Creek Timberwolves!" the announcer's voice boomed, and the crowd roared its support.

The kickoff line went out again, and Cooley managed to return the ball fifteen yards before they were brought down.

"Come on D-line! Let's hold 'em!" I shouted. The clock still showed less than two minutes and Cooley worked the ball, pulling off a good play which got them another first down. It didn't matter, though, because time was on our side tonight, and when the final buzzer blared, the defense had kept them from scoring again.

"Timberwolves come off victorious in their first conference game, beating the Mountain Lions twenty-seven to seven! Let's hear it for our Timberwolves!"

The masses thundered their approval as we lined up on the fifty-yard line to slap hands with the other team.

"Good game, good game," I greeted the players as we passed by, before running to join our team on the field for the customary after game pushups. We gave a shout and quick huddle before returning to the edge of the grass to sing the school fight song to the waiting crowd, as was our tradition.

The fans clapped along with us and cheered loudly when we were done. We headed to the locker room.

"Chase Walker," the announcer's voice came over the loud speaker, and I turned toward the press box in surprise, wondering what was going on. "Nikki Wagner says, yes, she will go to Homecoming with you next week."

"It's about time!" I hollered back, searching for her among the cheerleaders as laughter broke out through the dwindling onlookers.

She was standing there with a pretty blush, waving at me.

I pointed at her with a warning finger. "I'll deal with you shortly." I grinned and turned to go toward the locker room.

"She's just barely answering you for homecoming?" Brett said at my shoulder. "You asked her weeks ago."

"I know. I think she delights in torturing me for some reason. She thought it was funny I asked her so early, but I didn't want some other guy trying to sneak in and snag her."

"Yeah, because guys in this school are dumb enough to steal the main squeeze of the star quarterback." He rolled his eyes.

"Don't you be giving me any smack. You asked Tana a week later. It's not that big of a difference."

"Except school had actually been going for a week when I did it. You asked Nikki on the first day."

"Hey. It's my senior year. I want everything to be perfect. I got the girl I want—now I just need to get that state ring. Life is finally starting to work out, you know?"

"I get it. It's going to be amazing. I can feel it."

Nikki, my family, and Greg, were waiting for me by the gate to the field house when I came out. I walked over to them, giving the ladies hugs and shaking the guys' hands as they congratulated me on a good game.

"You're doing awesome, kid," Greg said.

"Thanks," I replied as my mom beamed. I knew she was glad Greg had kind of started growing on me during the summer. He really was as great as everyone said he was, and I was happy my mom had him in her life. It was nice to see her smiling again.

"Enjoy your date tonight. Don't stay out too late," my mom said, embracing me one more time before they left me alone with Nikki.

She stepped forward and kissed me softly on the lips. "Oh dear. You smell terrible."

I laughed. "Let's go to your house so I can get showered then." It was fortunate her mom let me do that, since it saved me a trip all the way to the ranch and back for our Friday night dates. I loosely draped my arm around her shoulders, and we made our way toward the team parking lot.

"You were amazing tonight."

"The team was amazing," I corrected her. "I can't do it without the rest of them."

"You know what I mean. Take the compliment. You're fabulous, and you know it."

"I have no problem listening to you tell me how fabulous I am." I grinned, and she shoved at me as I fumbled for my keys in my pocket.

"What the . . . ," I trailed off as I looked to where I'd left my truck parked. It was still there, but completely covered from one end to the other in plastic wrap.

There was a big sign on the driver's side door that had the word 'YES' written on it.

"You're so dead," I said, and she squealed and took off running.

She was actually pretty quick as she ducked and ran between the few vehicles which were still scattered about, but I managed to catch her right next to my truck and pinned her there.

"You're gonna get me all sweaty," she whined, squirming.

"You deserve it." I laughed, pressing against her harder. "You already had the announcer respond for you. You make me wait weeks for your answer, and then you do this too. Why?"

"I wanted to make sure you got the message." She smiled up at me innocently.

"Which message is that? The one proving I'll hang around for weeks waiting for you like a puppy on a string?"

"No. The one that says you're worth saying yes to twice."

I let my gaze run hungrily over her before returning to her face. "I wonder what else I could get you to say yes to?" I muttered, my voice low.

"You're not understanding."

"Understanding what?" I was confused.

"The yes from the announcer was for homecoming. The yes on your truck is for you."

"For me?"

"You told me—all those months ago by the creek— when I was ready I'd have to be the one to give you the go ahead. I'm telling you yes. I'm ready. I want you to be the one. I love you, and I want to share that part of me with you."

I was instantly on fire. "Are you serious? Like right now? Tonight?"

She shook her head, laughing. "No. I want it to be special for us. I was thinking we could plan something for after the homecoming dance."

I kissed her. Hard, hot, and fast. One week. I'd held myself in check all these months, night after night of heated make outs which left me hanging in massive frustration, and suddenly the thought of waiting one more week seemed endless.

I ran my hands up her body until they traveled into her hair, twisting and tangling as I angled her better against me. My tongue plunged into her mouth, and I moaned when she wrapped her arms around my waist, sliding them up my back.

"Go get her, Chase," someone called out, followed by a wolf whistle.

Our lips broke apart, but we didn't move, instead staring at each other. "I love you, Nikki." I smoothed her ruffled hair and chuckled. "I'm not lying when I say this will be the longest week of my life."

She nodded. "For me too." She looked to make sure we were completely alone before she spoke again. "My mom is taking the kids and going to see her sister, who just had a baby, in Texas next weekend. I'm supposed to stay at Tana's. I thought you could make arrangements to stay at Brett's, and then maybe we could meet at my house together."

At her house. I closed my eyes and let myself mentally picture it for a moment.

"Is that okay?" she asked.

"It'll be perfect." I kissed her again, before I pulled away. "Come on. Help me get this stuff off my truck so we can get cleaned up. I think there's a lot more kissing on the menu for tonight."

~Chapter Nineteen~

I paced the porch restlessly, my truck hidden in the dark recesses behind the house.

Where was she?

I looked at my watch for the billionth time, only to discover a minute had passed since the last time I'd checked.

"Walker, get some control," I mumbled to myself as I sank into the swing with a chuckle.

Yes, it was obvious—I was very excited for tonight. Today had been perfect—winning the homecoming game with credit for three touchdowns, plus two assists. Afterward, I went to the dance and had a fabulous, albeit distracting, time with Nikki, holding her body close to my own as we swayed to the music. It only served to ignite the fire for what was coming later—now.

I glanced at my watch again, wondering where she was. She was fifteen minutes late, but Tana lived clear out past the edge of town, so it would take her a little longer to drive here. I hoped she hadn't been caught sneaking away.

What if she changed her mind? I suddenly thought, feeling anxious over the idea.

No way. She'd been all over me tonight with her flirtatious touches, smiles and winks. We were both anticipating this evening together—I was sure of it.

I pulled my cell phone out of my pocket again, to see if she'd messaged, but there was nothing. I hesitated to text her, nervous it might alert someone else to what she was doing, so I held it in my hand instead, willing it to ring.

The sound of a car coming down the road caused me to let a sigh of relief, and I hadn't realized how worried I'd been. I stood and moved around the corner of the house to wait, pausing in disbelief as the vehicle drove on by.

It wasn't her.

Where R U? I finally messaged. R U ok?

I waited five more minutes before I jumped into my truck, pulling quietly out of the driveway. When I reached the highway, I turned in the direction of Tana's house, unable to help myself.

If Nikki had changed her mind, that was fine, but I didn't think she would leave me hanging without telling me. It wasn't like her. She knew I would listen to whatever her concerns were.

I had no idea what I was going to do when I got to Tana's house. I was fairly certain she'd probably fallen asleep while waiting to make her escape, but I wanted to make sure. I told myself if her car was parked safely in her driveway, then I would go back to Brett's, and we could discuss things in the morning.

Panic seized me when I saw the flashing lights in my rear view mirror. I pulled over, but the cop whizzed on past me at a high rate of speed. I moved back onto the road and followed after him, not caring I was speeding too.

The ambulance and fire truck were already there with their floodlights on, along with another officer parked next to the mangled mess of what used to be a red Volkswagen bug. I halted, frozen for a moment as my worst fears were realized—hoping I had fallen asleep and was having a terrible nightmare.

I leaped out and ran toward the accident.

"Hold it there, kid!" An officer stepped up to stop me.

"That's my girlfriend's car!" I shouted, pushing away before he caught me by the arm again.

"Hey. Listen to me," he said as he tried to detain me while I continued to struggle.

"Let go!" I yanked away.

He grabbed me again. "Listen. I'll let you go over there, but I need you to remain calm. The crews are working to extricate her. She hit an elk, and it went through the windshield. The car rolled several times. You need to prepare yourself."

"How is she?" A heavy tremor shook my voice.

"She conscious—calling for someone named Chase. Is that you?"

I nodded, unable to speak.

"It'll be hard for you to look at her. She's been cut up quite a bit from all the broken glass. Scalp lacerations bleed heavily so things may look worse than they really are. Do you have problems with seeing blood?"

"No." I tried to steel myself for whatever was coming, guilt and concern eating away at me. This was my fault. If she hadn't been coming to meet me, she'd never be here right now.

"Okay. Try to stay out of the way of the rescue crews and move wherever they tell you. Do you know how to reach her parents?"

"Her father's dead. Her mom is out of town," I replied numbly as he guided me closer. I could see remnants of the elk in pieces lying on the road.

I swallowed hard. There was a tarp over her body, and fire fighters were using a loud piece of equipment to cut through some of the metal.

"Why do they have her covered up?" I asked, hearing the fear laced through my own voice.

"It helps protect her from any debris from the extrication."

There was a popping sound as the door was breached and removed from the rest of the car.

The officer pulled me nearer as the plastic was moved away, revealing a person I couldn't even recognize. Blood was matted thickly through her beautiful hair, and there were several places of open flesh down the side of her face.

I choked and staggered backward. "It's bad," I whispered, hearing the horror in my own voice.

"It is. But she needs you right now. Are you up for this?"

I could only nod, and he guided me closer.

"Nikki, don't move. I wanted to let you to know Chase is here now, honey. He's going to sit right by you while the crews work on getting you stabilized and out of there, okay?"

"Chase?" she spoke, her voice gravelly with emotion. "I'm so sorry."

I felt myself wanting to crumble into a weeping mess.

Suck it up tough guy. She needs you, I mentally berated myself.

"Don't you worry about that right now, Nikki. Let's get you out of there so we can get you taken care of." I couldn't believe how brave I sounded.

She wiggled her bloodied hand. "Come closer."

I shifted toward the front of the vehicle where I'd be the most out of the way. I knelt down, as close as I could get and slipped my hand into hers. I couldn't help the trembling as she stared at me. Even her eyelashes were matted together with blood, but her eyes were clear, and they were scared.

"Hang in there, baby. These good people are doing all they can to help you."

She squeezed my hand like I was her lifeline, and I was happy to feel the strength there.

"I didn't see the elk until it jumped in front of me. I couldn't stop."

"Shhh. It's okay. No one thinks it's your fault."

No, it was all mine. I was the reason for all of this.

Tears leaked over the rims of her eyes. "I'm so sorry I missed our date."

"Don't be. There'll be other dates. Let's just worry about getting you better."

I watched as the ambulance crew set up two I.V.'s, and slipped a collar around her neck to stabilize it.

"Sir?" a woman spoke from behind me, and I turned. "We need you to come away from the vehicle while we pull her out. This officer over here would like to ask you some questions too, please."

I turned back to Nikki. "I'll be right over there, okay, baby? I won't leave you. Just do everything they say." I gripped her hand one more time before releasing her, moving to speak with the officer several feet away.

"I was wondering if you could help me with some of her pertinent information?" he asked, and I nodded, my eyes never leaving Nikki.

"What's your name?"

"Chase Walker."

"How old are you, Chase?"

"I just turned eighteen."

"What's Nikki's last name?"

"Wagner."

"And her age?"

"Seventeen."

"Do you know her birthdate?"

"March thirtieth."

"Her parents' names?"

"Her father passed away several years ago. Her mom is Justine Wagner. She's out of town, though, visiting her sister."

"Do you have her number?"

"Yes." I fumbled for my cell phone and scrolled through it for her contact. I was distracted when Nikki cried out loudly in pain, and it was all I could do to not rush to her side.

"The number?" the officer prodded me again.

"They're hurting her," I said, as she made another sob.

"I can assure you, they're doing their best to keep that from happening, sir."

"Then tell them to try harder," I growled angrily. "Give her something for the pain."

"They can't. She has a head injury, and they have to keep her alert. It's against their protocols."

I snarled as I paced away from the vehicle, dragging a hand roughly through my hair.

"I know you're worried, but I really need the number, son. We need to contact her mom."

"Let me do it," I said, turning around to face him.

He shook his head. "I'm in charge of getting the message to the family."

"Then stand here and watch me do it. She deserves to hear it from someone she knows and is familiar with, don't you think? You can talk to her when I'm finished."

The officer looked me over, before agreeing. "Okay, but no freaking out on me."

"I never freak out," I mumbled, suddenly wishing I had something I could smoke to help me mellow some, so I didn't have to keep faking this calm exterior. My whole world was threatening to collapse on itself.

I dialed the number for Nikki's mom, and let it ring.

"If you have to leave a message, tell her you need her to call you," the officer coached. "Does she turn her phone off at night?"

"I don't know!" I snapped, unable to control it any

longer. "I'm not sleeping with the lady."

"Sorry. It was a dumb question."

It went to her voice mail. I hung up.

"Why didn't you leave her a message?" the officer asked.

I leaned in to look at his nametag. "Look, Officer Barrett, what would you think if you woke up to a message like that in the middle of the night? Is that really what you want to hear, so you can sit there and panic over the million reasons why your daughter's boyfriend might be calling you at two o'clock in the morning?"

My phone started vibrating, and I looked down to see Justine's number on the screen. "Hi Justine," I answered.

"What's happened, Chase?" she spoke immediately.

"There's been a car accident," I said, my voice suddenly shaking uncontrollably. "Nikki's alive, but she's hurt really bad."

I heard her gasp, and I could hardly speak. "Here's one of the police officers." I handed the phone to him and turned to watch as Nikki—now on a backboard—was lifted and strapped to a waiting gurney.

I walked over, slipping my hand into hers while they wheeled her toward the waiting ambulance.

"Chase?" she asked, and the paramedic stepped to the side, allowing me to move in closer.

"Nikki, we're sending you to the hospital in Cooley by helicopter. The officers have set up a landing zone down the road. We'll drive you there as soon as it lands. Chase can meet you at the hospital."

As if on cue, I could hear the beating of the chopper's blades as it approached.

"I'm scared, Chase. I hurt really bad." Nikki's eyes looked at me pleadingly, as if I could stop her pain somehow, and I would've given anything to take it from her.

"You're tough, Nikki. I know you can do this."

"Can you fly with me?" she asked.

I shook my head. "No, but I'll get to Cooley as soon as I possibly can. I'll be right behind you, okay?" I bent and lightly kissed her blood-streaked lips. It was the only place that looked safe enough to touch.

"Time to go," the medic said, lifting the gurney into the waiting ambulance. The action caused my hand to be yanked free from hers.

"I love you, Chase," she called to me.

I mouthed the words back, knowing she didn't hear them because I was unable to move the sound past the knot in my throat.

I stood there, next to the mangled heap of metal in the middle of the road as I watched them drive away with my girl. I stayed there until the helicopter left the ground again, with her safely on board.

After getting my phone back, I hurried to my truck, turning around and headed toward Cooley. I only made it a mile down the road before I had to pull over because I couldn't see through my tears. Taking my phone from my pocket, I dialed my mom.

"Chase?" she answered groggily after several rings.

"Nikki's been in an accident, Mom. I need you to drive me to the hospital."

"Where are you?" she asked, instantly sounding awake, and I gave her directions. "Hang on, sweetie. I'll be right there."

I hung up and leaned over the steering wheel, finally giving my inner terror a voice.

"Please don't take her from me too," I pleaded to whoever might be listening. "I'll do whatever you want, just don't make me go through this again."

~Chapter Twenty~

I paced in the waiting room, hanging around for someone—anyone—to tell me something. The lady sitting behind the glass at the desk eyed me again, as if she were getting annoyed. I was ready to punch my fist right through that glass if people didn't let me know what was going on soon. I glanced at a fire extinguisher hanging on the wall. That would work too.

"Chase. Come sit down. You're driving everyone crazy." My mom patted the seat next to her.

"She's in there by herself, and no one is telling us what's going on. I told her I'd be with her."

"She's not alone. She got a team of people working on her. Let them do their job, son."

"What did her mom say?" I asked, referring to her recent phone call.

"She's getting packed up right now. I feel sorry for her. It'll be a long drive back from Texas."

"Did you tell her we would stay with Nikki? I don't want her to think she'll be abandoned."

"I told her. She's very appreciative and said to thank you for all your help so far."

I snorted. "What help? This is my fault. If it weren't for me, none of this would have happened."

"Are you going to tell me what was going on? I thought you were safely asleep at Brett's house." She arched an eyebrow.

I sighed, plopping into a seat. "She was sneaking out from Tana's to meet me at her house."

My mom picked at some imaginary lint on her pants. "I see. How long has this been going on?"

I laughed sardonically. "It hasn't. Tonight was going to be the first time."

"Really?" She turned to stare now. "I have to say I find it surprising, given how close the two of you've been."

I shrugged as if it were no big deal, as if I hadn't been after her for months. "Nikki's different. She was worth waiting for."

My mom squinted, looking at me closely. "You're in love with her, aren't you? I mean really in love, not just some teenager puppy I'm-so-cool-with-my-girlfriend type of affection."

I wiped my hand over my face before dropping it into my lap. What an awkward conversation to have with my mother.

"When did it happen?" she asked, reading my silence perfectly.

"Quite early, actually."

"Does she know how you feel?"

"I hope so. I tell her every day." I gave an exasperated grunt.

"And does she feel the same about you?"

"She says she does, and I believe her."

"Have you talked about your futures together?"

I knew she was trying to distract me, but it was okay. I needed to talk to someone about her.

"A little, but not much."

"What kind of stuff?"

"We talked about going away to the same college together. She wanted to see what scholarship offers I might get, and if she could follow me there."

"How do you feel about that?"

I rubbed my palms on the knees of my pants and stood up. "I'm totally down with it."

I started pacing again, unable to help myself.

"That could be hard on you—new life, new school, new girls to flirt with. They like the football players, you know? You think you could stick with her through all the attention?"

I lifted my hand in a helpless gesture before dropping it to my side. "Well, I would hope I'm not a complete jerk, since I was planning on asking her to live with me if things worked out."

"Chase. You're only eighteen and still a senior in high school. Don't you feel you're a little young to think about things like moving in with someone? Go out and live your life. Have a chance to enjoy it before you settle down."

I turned and looked at her. "And what if I miss catching the one person who really makes me happy because I did that? I know I'm young, Mom, and I'm honestly not trying to rush. These are only a few things I've thought about. That being said, the girl all busted up in there makes me feel better than anything I can ever remember. She helped me get through the hardest thing I've ever had to go through, and now I'm going to do the same thing for her." I raised my voice. "That's if someone will tell me what's going on, and let me in there with her!"

"If you don't calm down, they're going to call security and throw you out. Come on, son. Reel it in a notch."

The doors of the emergency room opened, and a man clad in scrubs came out. "Are you the Wagners?" he asked.

"No, the Walkers." My mom stood and shook his offered hand. "I'm Tori, and this is my son, Chase. He's Nikki's boyfriend. Her mom is on her way back from Texas. I told her I'd keep her informed of what's going on. She called the hospital and gave permission for me to make any critical medical decisions on Nikki's behalf."

"Very good. I'm Doctor Brannen." He gestured for us to sit together in a grouping of chairs, and I felt my pulse rate shoot up. "Nikki has some very serious injuries. I've looked at the results of her CAT scan, and she appears to have fractured her spine in the lower lumbar area. The spinal cord is intact, but there's quite a bit of swelling and deformity around the area. I did an exam, and she has no sensation or feeling below her waist."

I couldn't help the gasp that escaped my lips, lifting my trembling hand to cover my mouth.

No, no, no, this can't be happening, the words reverberated through my mind.

"Does that mean she's paralyzed?" My mom asked the hard question I couldn't put a voice too.

"It could, but we won't really know anything until the swelling goes down and relieves the pressure on the spine. We also need to operate to stabilize the vertebrae, but we won't be able to do that either until the swelling goes down. The next few days will be very crucial to her recovery.

I stood up and walked away, suppressing the urge to vomit. How could this be happening? She was a cheerleader. She couldn't end up paralyzed—it would devastate her. It would devastate me.

I turned around. "Can I please see her now?"

He nodded. "Yes. Once we made sure she didn't have any internal head injuries, we gave her something to help with the pain, so she's kind of out of it from the sedation. She has several large lacerations on the left side of her face which need to be closed. The plastic surgeon is coming in so we can get them sewn as nicely as possible for the time being, but she'll probably have some significant scarring."

I can live with scars, I thought. *I just need her to be alive.*

"So what's the plan from here then?" my mom inquired.

"As soon as we get her stitched up, we'll admit her to a room. We'll be giving her heavy doses of steroids to help the swelling go down quickly so we can get her to surgery and stabilize the fracture. Hopefully it will take only a day, but maybe two depending on how she progresses. She'll be in a lot of pain during this time, though, so she'll be on medication for that as well. Lots of sleep is good for her right now."

"Okay. Her mom will be able to get here before she goes into surgery then." My mom breathed a sigh of relief as the doctor stood, and we followed him into the emergency room.

He led us through the bustling people to a large room with a sliding glass door marked as Trauma One. I felt sick all over again when I saw Nikki lying there on the backboard. She was hooked up to several monitors, and an oxygen mask was over her face. Her breathing was deep and even suggesting she was asleep, which made me feel better for her.

Most of her clothes had been cut away to reveal her body for closer examination. What was left was stiff and brown with dried blood..

My mom grabbed my hand and squeezed, tears welling up. "Oh, Chase. I'm so sorry."

A nurse stood next to Nikki with a basin, gauze, and bottles of sterile water. "I'm Anna," she said as she removed the block which had been keeping Nikki's head secured to the board. "I'm getting ready to clean her up a little so the plastic surgeon can see what he's dealing with. Are you her family?"

"Family friends. My son is her boyfriend," my mom explained again. "Her mom is on her way home from

Texas."

I went to the other side of the bed, slipping my hand into Nikki's and rubbed my thumb over her skin.

"Chase," she mumbled immediately, but her eyes stayed closed.

I leaned next to her ear. "I'm here, baby. Go to sleep and rest while you can. They're doing their best to get you taken care of. Your mom is on her way home too. Hopefully she'll be here tomorrow."

"Don't leave me," she whispered.

"I wouldn't dream of it. I'll have the doctor stitch our hands together if you'd like."

She smiled then, not very big, but it was there nonetheless. "I love you, Chase."

"I love you too, baby. Go back to sleep. The doctor will be here soon to take care of your face."

She frowned a little. "Do I look bad?"

How could I answer that?

"You look like you've had a pretty rough night, but it's nothing some washing and stitches won't help. Don't worry about any of that right now."

She mumbled something I couldn't understand, and she drifted off again.

"She probably won't remember much of this later on," Anna spoke up. "A lot of accident victims don't remember this part. I think it's the brain's way of protecting itself."

I grunted. "I wish mine would do the same. I could certainly live without remembering her like this."

My mom patted me. "You're doing great. This is the worst of things, honey. Things will get better from here on out."

Unless she can never walk again, I thought. *I wonder how she will feel about me then, knowing I put her in a wheelchair for the rest of her life?*

I couldn't imagine her in a situation like that.

Images of the girl who'd been tossed into the air and went tumbling in flips and cartwheels across the gym floor filled my mind. This couldn't be the same girl I'd held in my arms a few short hours ago as we swayed together on the dance floor, touching and caressing one another—the girl I should have been holding right now, wrapped together in her own bed.

I clenched my teeth, kicking myself for my selfishness. My desires had brought this tragedy.

"Would you like to sit down?" Anna gestured to a chair and a rolling stool.

"I'll take the stool," I said to my mom, wanting her to be more comfortable in the chair.

She pushed it over, and I sat, leaning my head on the bed near Nikki's and my clasped hands. I didn't know how I would ever be able to make this up, but I did know one thing—I wasn't leaving her side until I helped her get better. If it meant I had to quit the team, school, college, whatever, I would do it. I owed it to her.

"Sounds like we're having a hard night in here," a new voice said, and I looked up to see another doctor in the doorway. He made his way over to Nikki, and the nurse stepped back so he could do his examination. He reached up and pulled a pair of latex gloves from a box on the wall, putting them on while he studied her.

"Nikki." He gently shook her shoulder, trying to rouse her, and her eyes flickered open. "Hi, Nikki. I'm Dr. Patrick, the plastic surgeon on call tonight. I'm going to take a look at these cuts on your face and sew them up for you. Okay?"

"Thank you," she whispered, sounding exhausted. "Can Chase stay with me?"

The doctor turned to me. "Are you Chase?"

I nodded.

"Do you have a problem with seeing her get stitches?"

"No. I can take it."

"Then I guess he can stay," Dr. Patrick replied to Nikki with a smile.

Nikki slept again, and the doctor and nurse began to set up something called a sterile field, covering her face and head until only her injuries were still exposed. They laid out several items including different needles and threads.

"She won't feel this, will she?" I asked, not wanting her to go through any more discomfort.

"She won't feel a thing after we numb her up," Anna assured. "We'll give her a local anesthesia."

I sighed and laid my head back on the bed next to her. I was suddenly so very tired.

"Chase? Do you need to go home and get some rest?"

"No," I said, not moving.

"She'd understand. You've been up all day and all night."

"I told her I wouldn't leave. I meant it. You can go if you would like. I'll be okay."

"I'll wait with you until they get her situated in a room."

"I'm not leaving then either," I said, feeling a stubborn streak coming on. "I'll sleep in a chair in her room or something."

"They actually have a couch in the room you can lay on," Anna spoke up.

"Perfect."

To her credit, my mom didn't argue with me. We sat silently watching the doctor stitch Nikki's skin back together as the nurse assisted him. I was glad to see the gaping wounds being closed, and the shape of her face returning to somewhat normal despite the swelling and stitches. They wrapped that side of her face and the rest of her head in fresh bandages, covering her dirty matted hair beneath.

"Okay. She's looking really good," the doctor spoke to my mom. "She'll have some thin scar lines when she heals, and they'll be red at first but eventually should fade out nicely. Hopefully she'll be able to cover it up fairly well with makeup, but if it bothers her too much we can readdress those issues if she'd like."

"Thank you for all your help," my mom said, shaking his hand after he removed his gloves.

"No problem. Happy to do it. They should be coming in to move her to a room soon. You all have a good night." He smiled and left.

I marveled how this was all in a day's work for these people. They were used to seeing this kind of thing all the time—like it was no big deal. It was a big deal to me, though, and I was going to see to it she had all the support she needed from now on.

~Chapter Twenty-One~

The sun filtered through the leaves of the trees, casting flickering shadows over Nikki's face as she lay in the grass beneath me. I bent to lightly kiss her lips again, listening to the sound of her increased breathing mingle with the sound of the creek and the soft breeze in the air. I lifted my face to look at her, my heart swelling with feelings.

She smiled tenderly. "I love you, Chase."

"I love you, too," I whispered, stroking my hand across her cheek and then her neck. I paused to trace her collarbone, marveling over how silky her skin felt under my touch, before I moved to replace my finger with my mouth.

I moaned when she arched her back and ran her fingers into my hair. I kissed farther down her body. This beautiful girl was mine. She belonged only to me. I slid my hands over her perfect figure, enjoying the way she moved in reaction to my touch.

I found another spot to attack and grinned when she called out my name. "Chase," her voice was a little deeper and huskier. "Chase."

Someone shook me, and I woke with a start, sitting up to find Nikki's mom staring at me with a concerned look. The beeping of Nikki's heart monitor was still going strong, and reality came crashing back in.

I sat up on the edge of the couch and hunched over, grabbing the sides of my head as I closed my eyes in despair. I'd been dreaming—dreaming of being with

Nikki while she was laying sedated a few feet away in the hospital bed I'd put her in.

What kind of freak was I?

Justine joined me and slipped an arm around my shoulders. "How you holding up, Chase?"

Sighing heavily, I tried to wipe the guilt I was feeling from my face. "I've been better, but still doing better than her."

I glanced to where Nikki, unmoved since the last time I looked at her. "How was your trip?"

She leaned against the couch. "Exhausting. Excruciating. I'm so glad you and your family were here. Your mom took the kids for me tonight, and I drove your truck so you'd have a way to get home. Your Grandpa and Greg are coming tomorrow to drop off my car. Your family has been amazing, as usual."

"They love you too," I replied. "I think having you all out to the ranch for the Fourth of July barbeque secured your place as a family favorite forever."

We both smiled at the memory, and I wished we could return to that night filled with sparklers, pie eating contests, and games. Life was so simple in that moment. I was happy my mom and Justine had hit it off, becoming best friends. My reasons were purely selfish, of course. They liked each other which meant Nikki and I got to spend more time together too.

"How's she been?" she asked, dragging me from my thoughts.

"Just like this since they admitted her. I think the drugs keep her from moving too much while they wait for the swelling to decrease."

She nodded and stood, going to place her hand on the top of Nikki's bandages. She bent to kiss her forehead. "I'm here now. I love you, sweetie."

Nikki didn't move, and I cast my gaze to the floor, the guilt eating away at me again.

"Why don't you go home for a while, Chase? Your grandma had dinner cooking when I dropped the kids off, and it smelled great. Go eat, sleep in your own bed, and get cleaned up. You can come back in the morning."

I shook my head. "I promised her I wouldn't leave."

"I know, but she would be furious if she woke up and saw you looking like you do. I'm here with her now. If she wakes, I'll tell her I made you go home to get some rest. She'll understand."

I opened my mouth to argue.

"Please, Chase. Let me spend some alone time with my daughter. Hospitals bring up difficult memories, and I want a bit of one-on-one time with her."

She gave me a pleading look I couldn't deny, no matter how much I wanted to. I knew she was remembering her husband's illness. I stood, and she dug into her pocket, handing me my keys. I took them and leaned over to kiss Nikki.

"I'll be back first thing in the morning," I whispered near her ear.

"Thanks, Chase," Justine said, as I passed by.

"Call if you need anything. And if she wakes up, please tell her I love her, and I'll be here as soon as I can."

"I will," she replied with a soft smile, and I left the room.

I hated leaving, feeling like I was going back on my word to Nikki. I'd already let her down dreadfully. I didn't want her to wake up and see that I'd done it again.

When I got in my truck, the gas gauge showed it was time for a refill, so I pulled into the first station I passed, groaning when I saw Chad and Wes coming out of the store with a case of beer.

"Dude!" Chad called, coming over to clap me on the back. "What are you doing in these parts?"

They must not have heard about Nikki's accident yet. "I could ask you the same thing."

"My buddy works here, and he sells to us," he explained, motioning to the alcohol. "You want to come party with us tonight? You look beat, man."

"I can't. I've been at the hospital all day. Nikki was in a bad car accident last night." I started the pump and left it to go into the store and get something to drink.

"What?" Wes said as they followed. "Is she okay?"

"She's sedated right now, but she broke her spine and needs surgery. She might be paralyzed from the waist down. They don't know yet." It made me sick to speak the words.

I opened the door and went inside.

"Man, that sucks. Anything we can do to help?" Chad asked.

I shook my head. "Not unless you can get rid of these awful memories in my head. I just need to go home and sleep."

Chad went to the register. "Drake, take care of my friend, Chase, here. Whatever he wants, he gets." He placed a twenty down on the counter.

"You don't need to do that," I said.

"Bro's take care of each other. You're our guy, Chase. Let me do this for you." He stared at me intently.

"Fine," I agreed after a moment, walking over to give him a fist bump. "Thanks, man."

"No worries. We'll try to come see Nikki tomorrow."

I nodded. "Sounds good. Catch you later."

I watched as the two left and climbed into Chad's car.

"Chad's a great guy," Drake spoke up.

"Yeah, he is."

"What can I get for you?" He placed his hand on the twenty.

"I need to pay for the gas on island three."

"Anything else?" He arched his eyebrow, and I knew what he meant.

I paused, wrestling with myself, but I lost the battle. "Throw in a case of beer too."

He smiled widely. "Will do."

I pulled my preferred brand out of the cooler while he rang things up and paid the difference Chad's twenty didn't cover.

"Have a good night," Drake said as I left the store.

Not a chance, I thought, giving him a nod because I didn't trust myself to say anything.

I drove straight to the creek, parking in the very spot I'd been dreaming about earlier. We'd come here on several different occasions during the summer. We never brought food again—mostly we made out like crazy. There were a few times we enjoyed playing in the creek too. We'd gotten pretty frisky with each other one day, and I'd thrown her in to cool her off. She stood up, her clothes clinging to every inch of her. I laughed as she grabbed and pulled me in with her. The hot kissing session had continued in the water too. I couldn't get enough of her.

The smile slid from my face as I pushed the memory aside. I got a beer and cracked it open, guzzling most of the can before I paused for a breath. I leaned over the steering wheel as I watched the water rippling in the moonlight. Everything was so peaceful looking, not like the churning turmoil going on inside me.

I finished the beer and took another one.

The images of Nikki all bloodied and mangled in the wreckage of the car popped through my head.

I knocked back this one too and went for a third, but the thoughts wouldn't stop.

She'd been coming to see me—to be with me. I should've told her no . . . told her we would wait longer to make sure she really knew what she wanted. But no.

I'd been in too much of a damn hurry to move things along. I'd been ready to take her the moment she'd spoken the words. Hell, I'd been wearing her defenses down for months.

I couldn't get over the fact if I had said no she wouldn't be lying in a hospital bed right now. It would have hurt her feelings if I'd reject her after an offer like that, but at least she would be whole, uninjured. Even if she hated me afterwards, it would've been worth it—to know she was okay. What was that saying about hindsight being twenty-twenty?

I finished the third beer and reached for another.

You shouldn't be doing this either, a tiny voice rose in my subconscious mind, and I shoved it back down where it belonged.

I was through being good. I'd tried to move on and live my life, and all I'd accomplished was hurting the person I loved most in the world. I was going to drink until every one of these voices in my head shut up. Good or bad, I didn't want to hear them anymore. I was sick of trying to be something I wasn't sure I was cut out to be.

Maybe I really was the bad kid, the player who smashed any girl who would give him the time of day, the kid who was constantly stoned out of his mind.

Was that really so awful? It saved me from having to deal with complicated lifestyles. I could simply coast along and exist, not caring about anything. There was nothing wrong with that. I didn't care if the people around me understood or not. Let them judge who they thought I was.

If this was what living a real life was going to feel like, then I didn't want it. I was done with this bull. I was going to do whatever I wanted, whenever I wanted, and no one was going to stop me.

I cracked open another beer, knowing I was getting

sloppy drunk and completely plastered.

"I don't care!" I shouted out loud to the stars in the sky. "This is who I am so deal with it!"

I tipped the beer and drank until I felt like I was drowning. I wanted to drown. I just wanted it all to go away.

Removing the can from my lips, I wiped my mouth with the back of my hand. "I don't care anymore," I said again, repeating my vow.

Liar, the stupid voice inside me spoke again. *You care too much.*

~Chapter Twenty-Two~

The sharp pain in my head caused me to abruptly come alive with a groan. I shielded my eyes at the bright sun burning my eyes.

"Crap!" I grumbled. It was daytime. I must've passed out and spent the whole night here. I reached for my phone to check for messages. It was dead.

I got out of the truck, first looking for a good place to relieve myself from the after-effects of my binge drinking. Afterward, I started crushing all the containers I'd emptied. My head pounded in agony with every single movement I made.

I emptied the remaining cans from the box, and broke it down—shoving it under the seat with the smashed cans until I could dispose of them. Now I needed to figure out what to do with the full cans. I looked around, my eyes settling on the creek. Walking along the edge, I searched until I found a place in the rocks where I could sink the cans into the water, keeping them nice, cold, and hidden for a later date—if the need were to ever arise.

I stumbled back to my vehicle, leaning against it as I fought a wave of nausea which threatened my stomach. I rubbed my face as I tried to collect my thoughts. I needed to get home and shower so I could get back to Nikki.

Fumbling with my keys, I managed to start the engine and head for home. Every bump in the road made my brain feel like it was sloshing against the insides of my skull. This was definitely a plus in the reasons-not–to-drink category. I forgot how fun hangovers could be.

I'd barely placed the truck into park when the front door swung open, and my mom came running from the house. She opened the driver's side and threw her arms around me.

"You're okay! Oh my gosh, I'm so relieved." She embraced me tightly. "You're in so much trouble, mister. Where have you been? We've all been worried sick about you!"

"Sorry, Mom." I hugged her back. "I went to sit by the creek last night after I left the hospital, and I fell asleep. I didn't wake up until now, and my phone is dead."

I turned my head away from her as I spoke, hoping she wouldn't be able to smell any alcohol on my breath.

"I didn't think anything was wrong until this morning. I assumed you had spent the night at the hospital. When I couldn't reach you, I called Justine's number, and she said you had come home last night. I was terrified you'd been in an accident yourself."

"No. I'm all right," I gripped her tighter. "I'm sorry I scared everyone."

"I better call and tell her we found you. Poor Nikki was beside herself with worry."

"Nikki's awake?" I asked, my heart sinking.

Mom followed as I hurried from the truck and up the steps to the house.

"She's been in and out of it most of the morning according to her mom. She keeps asking for you."

I actually growled under my breath, wishing I could punch myself for not being there on time. "I need to get back there."

"I'll make you some breakfast while you're getting cleaned up."

My stomach recoiled at the thought of food. "Don't trouble yourself. I'll pick something up on the way."

"It's no trouble at all. I'll pack you some stuff to go so you have something for the rest of the day as well."

I sighed before I agreed. I might as well give in because she wasn't going to relent.

"Chase!" an excited cry reached my ears as Nikki's little sister, Clara, ran down the hall toward me.

I picked her up and swung her around in a circle, despite how it made my head feel. "How's my pretty girl?" I asked.

"I'm okay. I missed you." A small knot formed in my throat.

"I missed you too. I'm glad you're home."

"Will you take me to see Nikki today?"

"I wish I could, but I can't. The hospital won't let you in right now."

She looked disappointed. "But I drew her a picture."

"Well, then go get it, and I'll take it to her for you. How's that?"

She grinned widely and nodded. I put her down so she could leave.

"Those kids adore you, you know?" my mom said.

"I feel the same about them."

"Your dad and I should've had more kids. You'd be a good big brother."

I wasn't in the mood to correct her and tell her exactly how wrong she was. "I need to get in the shower. Tell Clara to put the picture on my bed, and I'll take it." I didn't wait for her to answer before I headed up the stairs.

Pausing in the doorway, my gaze settled on Turk, and I realized I'd missed one of his feedings. I sat on the bed and dropped some flakes in under the plant roots.

"Sorry, I didn't feed you yesterday, little buddy.

Life's been on the rough side lately, in case you haven't heard."

There was a giggle from the doorway, and I glanced up to see Clara standing there. "Are you talking to your fish?"

I grinned—embarrassed that she'd caught me. "Yep. That's what grownups do, don't you know? We talk to stuff, about stuff, with stuff."

"Nikki talks to fish too."

"Yeah. I know she does. But that's because she's crazy."

Clara laughed again and came into the room for a closer look at Turk. "She is. I know because I heard her say it herself."

"Did you? What did she say exactly?"

"She was on the phone with Tana. Nikki said, "I'm crazy in love with Chase." She had this big goofy smile on her face like she always does when she talks about you. Do you love her too?" she asked innocently.

I paused, letting her words sink in for a moment. "I do. She's a great girl."

Clara's face grew somber. "Is she going to die?"

"No," I said a little too sharply, and she backed away. "No," I amended, softer this time. "But she's badly hurt, and she's going to need all of us to help her get better."

We sat there for a few moments in silence until I cleared my throat. "I need to go take a shower now. I've got to get back to the hospital."

"Here's the picture for Nikki." She handed me a piece of paper.

I looked down at the image, a drawing of a happy family standing together under the word love, with everyone's names labeled underneath—Justine, Clara, Timmy, Nikki, and Chase.

My heart clenched inside me. "Thank you, Clara. I'll

be sure she gets this. She'll love it."

She gave me another quick hug and turned to skip out. My eyes drifted back to her gift, warmness infusing at the thought of her including me in their family portrait.

I walked into the hospital room, finding Nikki there asleep by herself, and a moment of anger hit me. I didn't like her being left alone. I pulled a chair up close to her bedside, setting the vase of roses I bought on the phone stand and propping Clara's photo up next to it before I slipped my hand into hers.

"Chase," she whispered, opening her eyes to look at me with a tired glance.

"I'm sorry I wasn't here when you woke up."

"My mom explained where you were. It's alright."

I lifted her hand and kissed the back of it. "I missed you."

She stared at me. "Are you going to tell me where you were?"

I sighed and leaned into the chair, not wanting to answer the question.

"Did you use again?"

I shook my head, closing my eyes because I didn't want her to see through me.

"Did you get drunk?"

"Look, Nikki. Let's just say last night wasn't good, and I'm not too proud of my actions. I certainly didn't mean to disappoint you. I was having a hard time."

"Who'd you party with?"

"You really think I would go to a party while you're stuck here in this bed?" I could feel myself growing upset.

"Sorry. I thought if you were drinking it would be with some of your friends."

I fidgeted restlessly. "I wasn't with anyone. I went

to our place at the creek by myself and wallowed in self-pity. Not exactly the highlight of my existence, I know, but certainly what people have probably come to expect from me. You did."

"I wasn't trying to assume. I knew you'd been under a lot of pressure lately. I'm not blaming you for it. Heck, I'd probably join you right now if I could."

I felt like the biggest jerk, going on this way. "Nikki, I'm sorry I'm so touchy this morning. It's my guilty conscience talking. Don't worry about me. I'll get my head on straight eventually. Let's get you taken care of first."

"Worrying about you is what I do. I love you."

I kissed her again. "Then let me worry about you for a change. You've done enough for me. I owe you so much more."

"You don't owe me anything. You're here, and that's all I need."

"I plan on being here every second. I'm going to talk to coach about quitting the team. I'm sure he will understand."

"No!" she said sharply. "You won't quit."

"You need me more."

"Chase, I don't want you to quit the team. You know college scouts are looking at you."

"It doesn't matter. You're more important."

"I disagree. You need to be focused on your future."

"I can't think about my future when you're here like this. I haven't been able to concentrate on anything but you." I was getting more frustrated by the second.

"Chase. I'll make you a deal. You stay on the team, and I will do everything in my power to hit my physical therapy just as hard. I'll match your workouts hour for hour and try to get better. But I'm only going to do it if you stay on. If you give up, then I give up too."

"You aren't playing fair," I complained.

"I'm playing very fair. Now are you going to agree or what? I'm too tired to continue this conversation."

I rubbed my thumb over her hand. "You know I'll do anything you ask if it will help you get better."

"Good, then we're in agreement. You play football, I play therapy. Let's see who makes it to the end first, shall we? You to the state game or me walking. The loser has to take the other out for a fancy dinner."

"Doesn't that make us both winners?" I asked with a grin.

"No. I can't afford a fancy dinner like you can, so I'm going to have to beat you."

I laughed, feeling some of the pressure lift off my shoulders. "You're on, baby."

"Just remember, I'll know if you are cheating or trying to throw things in my favor. I won't have any of that."

"Go to sleep already," I teased. "What's a guy got to do to get some peace around here?"

She smiled and closed her eyes, squeezing my fingers tighter.

I watched her in silence, unable to drink in my fill of her with my gaze. She was so strong, and I loved her for it.

"Chase," she whispered.

"Yes?"

"I really am sorry I messed up our date."

My heart sank again. "I love you. Go to sleep."

~Chapter Twenty-Three~

Nikki was fast asleep again by the time her mom came back carrying some breakfast.

"Still sleeping, I see." She sat down on the couch against the wall.

"She woke up for a short while and visited."

"Good, I'm glad. She was really concerned about you."

I nodded, not quite able to meet her gaze. "Yeah, sorry about that."

She took a bite of her food, looking at me thoughtfully while she chewed. I felt like I had a big neon sign on my head flashing the word "guilty" all over it.

"Chase, you seem different somehow. Is there anything I can do to help? You know I love you like you're one of my own kids, right?"

I gave a soft snort, suddenly becoming interested in the tiles on the floor. I shifted uneasily.

"Talk to me. Maybe it'll help to get it out."

The tension inside me rose to an extremely uncomfortable level. I didn't know how to tell her what I needed, but I knew she deserved the truth.

"I know Nikki was meeting you so the two of you could spend the night together."

My head jerked up—reading her expression, looking for anger—but there was none.

"Nikki told me about it when everyone was trying to find you. She told me a lot of things—confidential things you've told her. She was worried you might have used some drugs and overdosed somewhere."

"So, all my secrets are out." I smiled wryly. "Is this where you tell me to get out, I'm not good enough to date your daughter?" I felt ill.

"No. This is the part where I reiterate my previous statement. I love you like my own child. You're part of our family now, and I'll do whatever I can to help you."

I laughed, and stood up, pacing away before turning around to face her.

"Why? I certainly haven't done anything to deserve that kind of treatment. I pressured your daughter to be with me, wearing her defenses down until she gave in. She's lying in this bed because of what I wanted her to do. If she never walks again it'll be my fault. Don't you understand?"

"That's not how I see it at all. I see two kids who have been together for months and have grown to have some very real adult feelings for each other. Nikki told me you never pressured her, letting her take things at her own pace. She said this was her decision."

I let out a groan of disagreement. "I pressured her every time I touched her, trying to fire her up so she'd want it as much as I did. I'm no saint and certainly not someone worthy of any sort of praise. Every time I think about her being here, it makes me so sick—I just want to vomit. She doesn't deserve this. It should be me, not her. The world can get along fine without a guy like me, but it needs all the people like Nikki it can find. She's so perfect—completely good, patient, and generous."

"If she's so wonderful, then why did she pick you, Chase?"

"That's exactly my point. She didn't want to go out with me. She called me a punk the first time we met. I wore her down, made her go out with me, and now look at her. It's like I destroy everything I touch."

Justine stood and came to place both of her hands firmly on my shoulders.

"Stop it, Chase," she commanded. "This is not your fault. It's an unfortunate accident. Nikki went out with you because she saw something she liked about you. That like turned into something much more. She feels this way because she loves everything about you. She wants all of you, the weaknesses and the strengths. That's how it works. She's not perfect, even if you think she is. She struggles with things like the rest of us. You can help her best if you stop blaming yourself. Otherwise your guilt is going to eat you up and take you someplace you've tried really hard to escape. Don't let it drive a new wedge between the two of you. She needs you now more than ever. It's time for you to be the strong one."

She didn't wait for me to reply, instead wrapping her arms around and hugging me tightly. I returned her embrace, knowing I was being selfish. What she was saying made sense. I couldn't see the hurt of the people around me because I was too intent on wallowing in my own.

She loosened her grip and stepped away. "We okay now?" She smiled.

I nodded. "Thanks for not being angry."

She returned to the couch. "I've been there. My husband and I got together in high school. I remember what it was like. There's no way I'd ever condemn someone else for feeling the same way. I've also learned since then that life can be way too short, so we need to try and make the best of it."

I sat down in the chair by Nikki's bed. "She's been trying to tell me the same thing. I guess she gets her good optimism from you. For some reason I don't have that. When my dad died, all I saw was darkness. I didn't know how to get past it. I'm not sure I wanted to get past it. I think maybe it was my way of hanging on to him."

"And there's nothing wrong with it. We all grieve differently, Chase. There's no right or wrong way. The important thing is to keep trying."

I snorted. "That's where I failed. I lost the desire to try. I didn't want to feel anything. It was too difficult."

"But you overcame it. Look at you. You had to do some things the hard way—like being arrested, and doing community service—but you survived it, didn't you? You changed some things, made new friends, and carved yourself a new life with a promising future. You need to start seeing the good inside yourself. It's definitely there. I happen to think you're your own worst critic."

"You're probably right. I think I've been living with my flaws for so long now, it's all I see sometimes."

"I don't believe that."

"Why?"

"I've watched you. You exude confidence. Every time you step on the football field I see a guy who knows he's in control. He knows he can conquer what's in front of him. It's in the way you walk, in the way you talk, even the way you act. No one messes with or gets in the way of Chase Walker. If I were to look up confident in the dictionary, your picture would be next to it."

I chuckled at the image she was creating, shaking my head at the analogy. "I'm glad I have you fooled."

"Have you ever wanted something and not gone after it?"

I thought about that, truly trying to come up with an answer and not finding one.

"See what I mean? When you make up your mind to do something, you commit to it completely. You go after it until you get it because you *know* you *can* get it. You don't stop until you have things the way you want them. You're confident."

Our conversation was interrupted by a nurse who came in.

"Good morning. We're getting ready to wheel Nikki down to CT and see how these steroids are helping her swelling. The doctor would like to get her into surgery as soon as possible."

"Okay, thank you," Justine replied while the nurse checked Nikki's I.V. and unhooked her from the monitors.

"Can we go with her?" I asked.

"Sure, you can walk down there with us, if you'd like. You'll have to wait outside of CT while we do the scan, though."

"All right. I just want her to know we're there with her."

"No problem."

Another tech arrived, and he began to release the brakes on her hospital bed.

"Nikki, can you hear me?" the nurse asked as she shook her shoulder gently.

Nikki opened her eyes slightly and mumbled something.

"We're taking you for a ride down to CT to run a scan and see how things are progressing for you."

"Okay." She looked between her mom and me with a tired expression. "Are you coming too?"

"Yep. You think I'm gonna let this guy go traipsing about this hospital on a joyride with my girl?" I winked at her, and everyone laughed.

"Ouch," Nikki said, moving her hand toward her chest. "That hurts."

"Sorry, baby. I didn't mean to make you laugh." I felt horrible.

"It's okay. I like hearing your snarky sense of humor. It makes me feel good." She seemed a little out of breath, but she smiled, reaching to clasp my hand for a moment as her bed rolled past.

Justine and I followed after her, and she slipped her arm in mine. "Thank you for being here with us, Chase. It means a lot." She leaned her head briefly onto my shoulder.

I covered her hand where it rested. "I don't want to be anywhere else."

The tech directed us to some seats in the hallway when we reached the room.

"I love you." I reached to give Nikki another caress. "We'll be right here."

"Thanks. I love you too," she said, and the tech pushed her bed through the doorway where there was another person in a lab coat waiting.

The door slowly closed behind them, and we sat down.

"How long do these things take," I asked.

"It shouldn't be too long. They just need to get some good shots of the area so the radiologist can read them."

"I wish they'd let us go in. I hate her having to do all this stuff alone."

Her mom put her arm around me and gave me a slight hug. "I'm glad you want to help her. She'll need that support. She's a tough kid, though, and a fighter."

I nodded and took my cell phone from my pocket. I'd changed the battery before I left home, and there were like a billion messages from everyone who had been trying to reach me. I started deleting them one by one as I read through them.

"Code Team One is needed in CT, stat. Code Team One is needed in CT, stat."

My head popped up. "Did they say CT?" I asked turning to see the stricken look of horror on Justine's face.

I jumped up and ran to the door, shoving it open. Nikki was on the table for the scan, and the tech and CT person were performing CPR.

"What's going on?" I yelled, the room suddenly spinning dangerously out of control.

"Sir, please step outside," someone said from behind me, grabbing my shoulders, pulling me to the left.

A barrage of people ran inside, pushing a large cart with paddles into the space.

"What's happening?" I asked again, shock settling over my system as I turned to the security guard who held me. "Please—someone—talk to me!"

"There's been a complication. Let the team do their work. It's the best thing for her."

Justine moved next to me, trembling, and I slipped my arm around her waist. "This can't be happening," she whispered, sliding her hands over her mouth.

The CPR continued as another person ripped Nikki's gown down from her chest. Someone else was placing a tube down her throat. "I'm in," he shouted, hooking a bag to the end of the tube.

A man turned with the paddles. "Charging. I'm clear, everyone clear."

The crew stepped back, lifting their hands from Nikki. The paddles were placed against her chest and her body arced hard against the table as the power shot into her.

"Checking for pulse," a nurse said, putting her fingers against Nikki's neck. "No pulse. Resume CPR."

The person at her head started bagging air into her, while the tech continued chest compressions.

"Charging again," the man called out once more. "Ready? I'm clear, everyone clear."

The people shifted away as Nikki was shocked

again, her body arcing high.

"Checking for pulse." We all waited with baited breath. "No pulse. Resume CPR." The crew went back to work again.

"Charging. I'm clear, everyone clear." He glanced around at everyone.

Another shock.

"Still no pulses. Continue CPR."

"Administering a round of drugs," the man at her head said, as everyone continued to work.

"Charging again. Everyone clear."

Shock.

"No pulse. Continue CPR."

Justine was sobbing on my shoulder. More people were running into the room to help. I could feel my whole body shaking, but I couldn't stop it.

"Why don't you two come sit back down in these chairs over here," the security guard prodded. "We don't need either of you getting faint or sick right now."

I realized I must've been holding the door open with my foot because it closed when I stepped away.

Anger suddenly overtook me.

"What the hell is happening?" I raged, my mind unwilling to accept what it was seeing. "She was fine a minute ago. What can happen in such a short amount time that she ends up like this?"

"I don't know, sir. But please try to remain calm. They're doing everything in their power to help her."

I laughed harshly. "Calm? You want me remain calm?" I strode down the hallway, suddenly feeling dizzy. I knelt down, planting my fist against the floor, staying there for what seemed like eons as the world dragged to a creeping pace around me.

"Chase," Justine called, and I turned to see her ashen expression, staring at the doctor who was coming through the door.

"Are you the Wagners?" he asked.

"Yes." Her voice shook.

I got up and began walking toward them.

"I'm not sure what happened, but I'm really sorry. We did everything we could, but she didn't make it."

"What?" I shouted, my vision going red as the whole world tilted. "That's not possible. She's seventeen years old. She has her whole life ahead of her still!"

"I'm sorry," he said again.

I grabbed the lapels of his jacket. "Stop being sorry, and get in there and fix her! You hear me? Fix her, and don't come out until you're done."

"Security is needed by CT," a voice behind me said, and I felt strong arms wrap around me like a vise grip. "Let go of him, son. You can't attack the doctor."

"I don't care," I yelled, shaking him. "He needs to do his job!"

The doctor simply stood there with an apologetic look, but he didn't try to move away.

I saw two other officers appear at the far end of the hallway. They ran quickly, grabbing me, pulling me away as I fought with them.

"Fix her!" I shouted again. "Fix her!"

They dragged me into a vacant room.

"You've got to calm down, sir!" They held me tight, twisting my arms behind me, pressing my face hard into the wall. "We don't want to have to call the police. Please try to understand."

I quit struggling and they released me. I swung my fist back, punching clear through the sheet rock.

"Not Nikki too," I cried as I sank to the floor. "Please God. Not her too."

I covered my face with my hands and sobbed uncontrollably, unable to stop the heart wrenching pain which shot through me.

No one said anything more, but I heard the door

open, and a second later, soft arms enveloped me. I looked up long enough to see her mom there, tears streaming down her face. I buried my head into her shoulder, letting her cradle me as the floodgates opened completely.

~Chapter Twenty-Four~

My life had turned into a horror movie. That must be it—I decided as I held Justine's hand and watched the casket which held the body of my girlfriend being lowered into the ground. The sound of sniffling and people shifting to wipe their eyes filled the air around me in the quiet cemetery. I couldn't cry anymore. The tears were always right there, but I forced them to leave, swallowing at the ever-present knot in my throat—the one I could never seem to make go away.

Everything was moving in a fog for me, different people passing through at separate times and spaces. I had been vaguely aware of my mom next to me, holding my hand one moment, and in the next, Timmy and Clara were sitting on my lap, their arms clasped around my neck. Justine was often present as well, but I could barely stand to look at her because she reminded me of Nikki so much.

The only constant presence I was truly aware of was Brett. Every second he wasn't required to spend in his own life, he was with me. He didn't say much, he was just there.

I didn't go to school, or practice the whole week after Nikki died while we waited for her funeral to take place. I couldn't stomach anything. No one asked why or when I intended to go back. No one said anything, actually. It was almost as if they were afraid I was a time bomb waiting to explode.

As for me I could only think of seven words.

Sudden death caused by massive pulmonary embolism.

They ran over and over in my mind like a freight train ever since I heard the official autopsy report. A simple thing, like rolling Nikki from the bed to the CT table had caused the blood clot to dislodge, and in a matter of a few seconds she was dead—taken away from me forever. Nothing could've been done to help her.

Even now, as her casket disappeared before my eyes, I couldn't wrap my head around all of it.

"I'm sorry. I can't stay any longer," I whispered to Justine. I released her hand and walked away, moving to where I'd left my truck. I heard someone following behind me, and I turned to see Brett. I shook my head. "I need some time to myself, okay?"

He stopped, and I could see the hurt on his face.

"I'll meet you at my house for the luncheon in a little while. I appreciate you being here for me. But I really need a few minutes alone."

He nodded, standing still as he watched me get in my truck and drive away.

I knew exactly where I was going, and I followed the familiar route until I was parked in front of the rest home. I'd been to this place several times, but always with Nikki. Her grandma hadn't been able to attend today because of her disabilities, but suddenly she was exactly the person I needed to see. I knew she couldn't talk, but I didn't need wisdom or words of advice. I wanted someone I could just be me with.

I stopped by the kitchen on my way and picked up a spoon and her favorite pudding from an orderly there.

"We're so sorry to hear about Nikki," he said, giving me the dish as he looked at the suit I was wearing. "Mrs. Wagner will be glad you're here. I know she would've liked to go to the funeral."

"Thanks," I mumbled, not knowing what else to say,

so I left.

"Grandma?" I called out as I entered the room, and she glanced up. Tears filled her eyes as she waved for me to join her.

I slid my chair up beside the bed, taking her dysfunctional hand in mine, rubbing my thumb over it.

"I brought your favorite pudding. I thought maybe you would enjoy the snack."

She waved it off, gesturing for me to set it on her nightstand.

I did as she asked, and she looked at me expectantly. "The funeral was very nice—lots of people and flowers. She was well loved."

She shook her head and pointed at me, placing her hand over my heart.

"I miss her so much I don't think I can stand it any longer," I choked out, and the tears I'd been holding back all day could no longer be restrained.

She nodded and gestured to her lap. I lay my head there on her small form as she ran her fingers through my hair, over and over again.

The house was packed clear full with a sea of people dressed in various shades of black. I stepped inside, trying to be as invisible as possible, not making eye contact with anyone while I made my way to the stairs. Wes, Chad, Brett, Tana, and Brittney were all crammed together on the large couch in the game room, staring blankly at the television which wasn't even on.

"You're here," Brittney said with an obvious relief, her eyes red from crying. She stood and came to me, followed closely by the others. "I'm so sorry, Chase," she whispered as she wrapped her arms around me, laying her head against my shoulder.

"Thanks," I mumbled, hugging her as I felt the guys clapping me lightly on the back.

"What can we do to help?" she asked.

I sighed. "You're already doing it." I squeezed her tighter before releasing her, turning to embrace Tana too and moving to plop down in one of the chairs.

I watched them return to their seats, seeming slightly uncomfortable, not knowing what to say. I knew they all missed Nikki too. She'd been a big part of all of our lives.

Silence followed, the awkwardness passing as I retreated into my own thoughts. It was enough for me that they were here.

Was this what my life was going to be like from now on? Sitting in a room full of people knowing the person I wanted to be with was never going to walk through the door? I'd been planning a future with her, and now there was nothing left. My dreams and thoughts were shattered before they'd really had a chance to begin.

I wondered if this was how my mom felt when my dad died, as if her heart was being completely pulverized. The pain was excruciating, and I didn't want to feel it anymore.

Chad excused himself and made his way down the hall. I caught up with him just outside of my bedroom, pulling him inside. I shut the door.

"Dude, you got anything on you that you can spot me? You know I'm good for it." I gripped his arm in desperation.

He glanced down, pondering for a moment before giving me a sympathetic look. "Even if I did, I wouldn't let you have it. Not in the state you're in."

I growled and shoved away from him, feeling angry. "You've practically begged me to join you at parties and now, when I really need it, you're not going to help me out?"

He looked away. "I'm sorry, Chase. I know you're having a rough time. I want you to feel better, but not this way. It would be too easy for you to take this the wrong direction, and I don't want to be standing at your funeral next."

I felt totally frustrated because I couldn't fault his sense of reasoning. He was right. I was in a bad place, and honestly, thoughts of suicide had crossed my mind more times than I could count.

I didn't care if it was a cop out. I'd been through this once before, and there was no way in hell I wanted to do it again. I was locking up my heart and throwing away the key this time. No more damage could be done if I couldn't be reached, because frankly, if this is what life had to offer me, I didn't want to live it.

"Forget it," I said roughly. There were other ways I could bring about the same results.

"You know we're here for you, right? There's a whole group of your peeps sitting right out there. We have your back, bro, anytime you need us."

I didn't want anybody else. I wanted Nikki.

"I'm really tired. Can you let everyone know I went to bed? I can't face any more people right now."

"Sure thing," he replied with a nod. "Text me later if you need to."

"Thanks. I will." I closed the door behind him. I took off my suit coat and belt while I kicked my shoes off, before dropping to sit on my bed. There was a soft knock, and I hung my head for a moment, desperately wanting to ignore it. I waited for a few moments, and the knock came again.

"Chase?" Brittney's voice spoke from the other side.

I walked over and leaned my head against the barrier between us, my hand on the knob, but I didn't open it.

"I'm afraid I'm not very good company right now, Britt."

"That's okay. I was just worried about you. I can

talk to you another time."

I rumbled out a soft sound, feeling badly for pushing her away when I knew she was hurting too. I opened the door, gesturing for her to come in and sit on the bed. She did, and I watched her while I began unbuttoning my dress shirt. I left it hanging open and slouched into the chair in the corner, waiting for her to say something.

"Chad said you wanted to go to sleep."

"Yeah, I'm pretty worn out."

She fumbled with the hem of her black dress lying around her knees. Her long, white-blonde hair fell forward around her face, and I could almost imagine her as a pretty angel in mourning sitting all dressed up in here.

It was weird having a girl who wasn't Nikki in my room, and it almost made me feel guilty.

When she looked up there were tears in her eyes. "I was walking down the hall and overheard what you asked Chad. I'm worried you're going to try something stupid."

I shifted uncomfortably. I must've been talking louder than I'd realized. I didn't know what to say. I peered over to where Turk swam in his vase. I couldn't deny anything.

"You need to keep remembering Nikki loved you, and she believed in you for a reason."

I glanced back at her, still not replying.

"She's not the only one who believes in you. A lot of us do." She hesitated. "I do too. You're a great guy."

I didn't know how to explain the inner turmoil I was feeling. I couldn't put my emotions into words. I was struggling, floundering. I knew she was trying to help. But there was really only one person who could reach me right now, and she was dead.

"Thanks for caring," I managed to mutter.

"I do care . . . a lot. If you ever need someone to talk to, vent to, or even scream at—I'm willing to listen."

"Thanks," I said again.

She stood and walked toward me placing her hand on my arm. "Be careful, Chase."

I nodded and patted her hand. She grasped onto mine, clutching it slightly before she disappeared out the door, closing it behind her. I leaned forward on my knees, thrusting my hands into my hair as I took a deep breath. I felt like I was suffocating, as if the walls were closing in on me.

I buttoned my shirt back up, slipped my shoes on and went quickly down the stairs. I glanced around for Justine, spying her coming out of the kitchen.

"You doing okay?" I asked her as I approached.

She nodded. "Under the circumstances, yes. Everyone has been so loving and supportive. How about you?"

"I need to get out of here for a while. Is it okay if I go hang out at your house?"

She stared at me sadly. "Are you sure that's the best idea?"

I swallowed hard, my tears mirroring her own. "I . . . I just need to feel close to her right now."

"Then go. I understand. You know where we keep the spare key. I'll be there in a little while."

I nodded and left, careful not to make eye contact with anyone as I went to my truck. I pulled my phone out and sent my mom a text so she wouldn't worry.

Going 2 Nikki's. B back later.

~Chapter Twenty-Five~

I took a deep breath before I turned the knob and entered her room, instantly on sensory overload. Everything was exactly the way she'd last left it. There were textbooks sitting on her desk, a couple pairs of her shoes tossed randomly in front of her closet, and several outfits thrown across the back of her overstuffed chair.

I wandered over to her bed and sat down, almost able to imagine she'd come waltzing through the door at any minute.

One of her vampire romance novels was spread open on her nightstand. Next to it was a picture of the two of us together on the Fourth of July, holding sparklers as we laughed. She loved the picture so much, she'd had it blown up and framed. I picked it up, absently tracing a finger over her happy face and wondered if we would've been so carefree if we'd known our time together was so limited.

I laid back on her pillow, closing my eyes and inhaling deeply as I caught a whiff of her scent clinging to it. Her perfume reminded me of days we'd spent together in the sun, kissing one another until we could hardly breathe. The memories were both sweet and exquisite torture.

Opening my eyes, I couldn't help the smile slowly spreading across my face. She'd taped a bunch more photos of the two of us on the ceiling over her bed. They were all silly, random, shots we'd taken, with either our cell phones or her small camera, but suddenly they were priceless. She was so alive in these images.

I studied each one of them as the late afternoon light dipped farther down the window, staring until it hurt too much to stare at them any longer. I shut my eyes, but the tears managed to seep through the lids anyway.

We were supposed to have been together right here in this very room. It would never happen now. It wasn't fair I was still here, and she wasn't. I felt horrible about everything and my apparent role in the situation. Not only had I lost her, but so had her wonderful family. There was no way I could make up for any of it.

"I want to be wherever you are," I whispered. "Please don't go any farther without me."

I wasn't sure how I was going to do it, but I was ready to find a way to join her.

Those same pictures greeted me when I woke, and I glanced groggily around the room as I tried to get my bearings. The morning sun was shining outside, and someone had covered me with a blanket. I realized I must've fallen asleep and spent the entire night. I hoped Justine let my mom know where I was so she wouldn't worry again.

Delicious smells were coming from the kitchen, and I got up to go apologize for staying.

"Morning," I greeted with a mumble as I made my way to the table and sat down, running my hands through my hair in an effort to tame it.

"Did you sleep well?" She turned from the stove and smiled. I could see she was tired and looked as sad as I felt.

"I guess. Sorry I crashed here like that."

"No need to apologize. I asked your mom if she wanted me to send you home, and she said to let you rest. Truthfully, I'm glad you're here with me. It makes things feel less . . . lonely."

I knew what she meant, but found it very difficult to answer her. I didn't know how to comfort either of us.

"Well, thanks for not kicking me out," I finally managed. "Is there anything I can do to help you with breakfast?"

"You can butter the toast while I finish cooking these eggs if you'd like."

I did as she asked, moving silently around the kitchen next to her. It seemed so weird to be here without Nikki, and for a moment I tried to pretend she was in the bathroom getting ready for the day while I visited with her mom. It was easy to do since it was a scene which had played out hundreds of times in the past. I enjoyed spending time here with this family. I loved them as if they were my own.

I thought about the decision I'd made last night and felt a slight twinge of guilt. I knew there were people who would mourn me if I left. I hoped they would understand why. I obviously wasn't as strong as everyone else was because I couldn't keep going on this way.

"Have a seat, Chase," Justine said as she slid a plate on the table. "I thought we could visit while Timmy and Clara are still sleeping. I figured I'd let them enjoy a late Sunday morning. Things have been draining for them lately too."

"I'm sorry it's been so hard on them." I stabbed at my eggs and took a bite.

"Again, there's no need to be sorry. It's not your fault."

I almost choked on my food as my throat went dry. How could she say something like that? It was totally my fault. I'd never forgive myself for my role in all of this. I didn't trust myself to speak so I continued eating, without making eye contact with her.

If she was waiting for me to respond, she didn't push the issue, instead eating in silence with me. When I was finished, I carried my plate to the sink and rinsed it before putting it in the dishwasher. Things were growing more strained for me by the minute and I hated it. I'd started feeling at home here, and now it was all being taken away. Everything was just plain awkward now.

"Thanks for breakfast. I guess I better get home." I dried my hands nervously on my wrinkled dress pants.

She sighed heavily and dropped her fork. "Don't go yet. I meant it when I said it was nice having you here."

I didn't know what to say to ease her pain.

"Actually, I found something this week I'd like you to see. I think it might help."

"What's that?" I asked.

She stood and motioned for me to follow. I did and she led me into Nikki's room, walking into the closet. She emerged with a book.

"This is Nikki's diary. I think you should read it."

I stared at the object she was holding, my heart picking up a beat. This book was part of Nikki—her voice, her insights.

"Are you sure?" I swallowed hard, knowing I wanted to read it. "I don't want to invade her privacy."

She stepped forward and placed the book in my hands. "Read it, Chase. She would want you to. You can stay in here. I'll call your mom and let her know what you're doing."

"Okay." She left and I locked the door so I wouldn't be disturbed, before making my way over to the chair in the corner. I sat down and stroked the cover, wondering how many times she'd held it while she recorded her inner most thoughts. I held it like it was a lifeline, both excited and afraid over what was hidden between the pages, knowing they would be the last words of hers I ever read.

I took a deep sigh and opened it.

The first part of it was filled with things that happened before we met, but I devoured every word, treasuring the piece of Nikki's world it showed, and who she was at that time. Here and there were pictures or special notes and papers she'd slid into it. I loved seeing all the images of her.

I laughed when I got to the part about her meeting me. I'd certainly made a less than stellar impression that first day. To say she'd been appalled might actually be a vast understatement. I was glad I'd managed to make her change her opinion.

There were a lot more memories of the two of us recorded. I loved getting to read her feelings from her point of view. I relived every moment with her in my mind.

I'd been reading for several hours when I came to a special place in the diary she'd sectioned off with a rubber band. I carefully slipped it off, surprised by what I found inside, and my fingers started shaking as I looked at the pages.

It was a letter she had written specifically to me.

~Chapter Twenty-Six~

This is a special part in my diary. I'm going to call it the Letter to Chase section. Sometimes there are things I want you to know, Chase, like how you're the guy I'm madly and irrevocably in love with. You make me so happy, that sometimes I feel overwhelmed with the need to tell you stuff. But when it's in the middle of the night, like tonight, I can't talk to you, so I thought it would be nice to write all these things down and maybe someday you and I can share them together. You'll probably laugh at me for doing this, but I don't care. My heart is full, and I need a place to put it all.

Let me start out by saying I really didn't want anything to do with you in the beginning. I thought you were a player—one of those kids who gets everything he wants in life, then discards it when he's done. I quickly learned I was wrong, and I shouldn't have judged you on preconceived misconceptions.

Somehow you wormed your way into my heart and made a home for yourself there. I've honestly thought you were a little crazy at times, but that's what makes you so lovable. You're both strong and tender. You're not afraid to march to the beat of your own drum. You make me laugh, and your kisses are like a piece of heaven on earth. I don't know if there really is any good way to describe you, except to say . . .you're just Chase.

Remember the day I fell during a stunt at cheer practice? I was okay, but I hit my jaw and cracked a tooth. My coach called my mom, and she got me an appointment with the dentist. You came and picked me up afterward to take me home, and we sat in the driveway for an hour kissing. You said you'd never kissed anyone whose mouth was deadened with Novocain before and told me you needed to experiment. You wanted me to tell you how much I could feel.

It felt funny because I couldn't sense things properly, but then you spent half the time kissing my neck, which made your little experiment total null and void anyway—not that I minded in the least! Ha, ha.

I want you to know I loved that kiss! I swear I could let you do that to me all day and never get tired of it. I made up my mind right then—I never want you to stop!

How about the night you took me out to dinner, and we had a discussion on middle names? You were determined to pry mine out of me, and since I always give in so easily I decided to make you sweat for this one. It drove you insane that I wouldn't tell! I laughed so hard. When you finally snatched my purse and fished out my driver's license I didn't realize what you were doing until it was too late. "Nikki Marie Wagner," you read out loud and told me it was perfect.

All I could think of was how much I loved hearing the sound of my name on your lips. It gave me goose bumps. Then you wrapped your arms around me and kissed me right there in front of everyone. I was blushing so hard, but I was the happiest girl on the planet.

But then you refused to tell me your middle name, so when we were walking out to the truck, I leaned up against it and tempted you with a kiss. You actually groaned when you thought I was grabbing your butt until you felt me lift your wallet right out of your pocket! You may have caught me quickly after I ran away with it, but I have to say I love your name too, Chase David Walker.

I was glad we had that night together, because I thought I might die during the two weeks in June when we didn't get to see each other during your football camp, followed by my cheer camp. Whose dumb idea is it to not allow cell phones at these things? I understand the need for building team unity, but this was just cruel and unusual punishment. I thought I was going to go crazy without getting to talk to you!

Oh, but the first night back together made it all worth it, didn't it? I was excited to go to the movie, but you came to pick me up and couldn't stop kissing me. We made it as far as the porch swing and spent the rest of the night in each other's arms until it was time for you to go home.

I remember you asked me what my plans were for college after I graduated. I told you I wanted to go wherever I could major in counseling or psychology and asked why you wanted to know. When you said you wanted to be wherever I was because being without me was torture, I thought my heart might explode with sheer delight.

Am I too young to be considering things like this in my life right now? I can't seem to get the conversation out of my head. I couldn't imagine anything better than being with you at college too. I love you so much.

I think you have an amazing future ahead of you. I've watched you at practice a lot. You're amazing! You'll get a scholarship for sure. I honestly think you're superstar material, and I hope I'm lucky enough to get to be with you for every second.

Oh, and you're the best boyfriend ever! Bringing me those roses at my cheer practice . . . be still my heart! When you said you saw them in the store, and *they were so pretty they reminded you of me, I think every girl on the squad swooned. I can't believe how sweet you are! I swear, every time I look at you it's like my heart is going to flip out of my chest or something . . . it races so fast. I don't even know how to describe it, except to say you make me feel the most wonderful things.*

I also have to say the Fourth of July has to go on record as one of the best days of the entire summer. I loved celebrating Independence Day with our families out at the ranch. The barbeque and pie was delicious, and the games and playing with the sparklers were so much fun.

The best part of the night for me, though, came at the town fireworks. I loved that you brought a blanket and spread it in an area away from everyone else. When you proceeded to kiss me during the entire display, I could actually feel the earth moving as the air exploded around us. Every time I opened my eyes, I could see the explosions in the air over your head and it was as if you were some mythical being creating this magical haven for just the two of us. You told me you loved me, like you do every day, but I never get tired of hearing it. You literally rock my world. I can't get enough. It makes me wonder if you know exactly how special you really are.

I've had several long visits with you about this. I know you get feeling discouraged about things which happened after your dad's death. I love that you feel you can come talk to me, but I hate seeing you hurt. I know you miss your dad so much and can tell you had a very close relationship. For some reason you can't seem to see yourself the same way I see you. It's as if you get hung up on your flaws, and you berate yourself until you feel so torn down you're miserable.

I wish you could see through my eyes. Just one

time is all it would take for you to know the kind of person you really are. Yes, you've had issues with drugs and alcohol in the past, and I realize sometimes it's hard not to turn back to those kinds of things. It's what became comfortable.

You've come so far, but you don't see it that way. You miss the lifestyle sometimes, so you feel it means you're not truly trying hard enough to change. I don't condemn you. It's natural for you to want to hang with your friends, but it's hard when they're doing things you're trying to leave behind. The temptation will always be there. I get it. I wish I could help with it somehow.

I want you to be happy. I wonder if I'm failing you somehow because you make me feel so good all the time. I don't know what I can do to make you feel the same way.

It's not that you aren't doing well, it's that you get down and don't seem to think you're worthy of the things you have. You are. You've worked hard for what you've got. I want to stand on the roof and shout to the world how wonderful you are.

Do you hear me, Chase Walker? I love you! You're wonderful! If there's one thing I wish you could truly know it's that I think you're pretty near perfect. The world became a blessed place on the day you were born. You're so strong, and you have such a good heart. I know you can conquer anything you set your mind to. And no matter where I am, or what I am doing, I'll always be your cheerleader, cheering you along just like you do for me.

Someday when you're old and gray, I'm going to look at you and the fabulous life you've lived and say, "I told you so! I knew you would rock the world!" And you will have to agree and tell me how right I am, won't you? Ha, ha! I know how much you'll hate doing that. But mark my words . . . Chase Walker is going places!

So stop looking at the past and all the things you can't change. They're done and over with. Now is the time for you to look to the future, grasp it by the hand, and decide where you want to go. I told you once before, and I'll say it again—this is your life, Chase. Only you can decide what it's going to be like. Don't let outside forces dictate it for you.

But whatever you do, I hope you'll always know I love you more than anything. You will always be with me wherever I go, because I hold you in my heart. You're a piece of my very soul. Please . . . don't ever give up.

Nikki

I could hardly see the words for the tears. It was as if she'd reached inside me and flayed me wide open. It was as if she knew . . . like she was here talking to me right now, coaching me, guiding me, and cheering me on.

Only I didn't know if I was strong enough to do what she was asking.

~Chapter Twenty-Seven~

The cemetery was quiet this early in the morning. I placed the fresh roses on her grave next to the dozen other wilting plants left here just two days ago. I stood very still staring at her name on the marker at the head of her plot, having a hard time believing she was here in this permanent resting place.

"So, I got your letter," I said. "Your mom found it and gave it to me." I struggled to speak, my voice catching with emotion. "I want you to know I really love you too—so much more than I could ever possibly show you.

"I guess I'm going to try to give you the only thing I have left, and that's my life. I've decided I'm not going to try to join you. After I read what you had to say, I feel like it would be letting you down if I tried to follow. I don't want you to think the things you tried to show me were in vain.

"I know you'd tell me I should be doing this for myself and not for you, but this is going to have to be good enough for a while because it's all I've got right now.

"On that note, I want you to know I've made a firm commitment to stay off the drugs and stuff. I was afraid to let them go before, and honestly I still am, but I'm going to sign up for Maggie's group session and learn the proper tools to help myself."

I swallowed at the knot in my throat, wondering for the millionth time why living had to be so hard.

"I'll do my best to make you proud, wherever you are. You're a piece of my soul too, and I will never forget you as long as I live. Thank you, for everything. I love you."

I stayed there for several long moments, having a hard time getting my feet to move from the spot. I finally forced myself to turn and walk away.

"Goodbye, Nikki," I whispered.

I hurried to my truck and drove away, fighting the urge to look back, my hands shaking against the steering wheel. I pulled into the lot at the school and parked, leaning my head against my arms. This was too hard.

Stop looking at the past, her voice echoed in my mind. *Look to the future.*

Sighing, I reached into my pocket and took out my cell phone, dialing a number.

"Hello?" Coach Hardin's voice came.

"Coach. This is Chase. I'm sorry I missed all the practices and the game last week. Is it still okay if I keep playing?"

"Of course it is. You never lost your spot. We've been holding it for you until you felt you could come again. Your mom and Grandpa both talked to me about it."

"They did?" I asked, surprised because no one had said anything to me.

"Yes. They've been worried about you. We all knew you needed some time to get over the initial shock of things."

"Thanks, Coach." I felt overwhelmed. "I'll see you at practice this afternoon then."

"Sounds good to me," he replied. "Glad to have you back, Chase."

I hung up and put the phone away, releasing a deep breath.

I got out and headed toward the school, staring at my feet as I walked alone, not really wanting to make eye contact with anyone.

"Hey, bro," Brett's voice said, and I looked up to find him standing with Brittney, Tana, Chad, and Wes. "We've all been waiting for you."

I couldn't speak as I saw my friends here, ready to support me even though they were dealing with their own grief too. I was going to get through this—*we* were going to get through this—together.

~Epilogue~
Four Years Later

The crowd was still going wild as the television reporter pulled me off to the sideline, shouting at me so he could be heard over the melee.

"Chase Walker, this has to be an amazing moment for you today, not only playing here in the college Fiesta Bowl in your home state of Arizona, but also scoring the winning touchdown in a very tight game. You've been an amazing quarterback, and there are already many bets on you being a first round pick for some of these scouting NFL teams."

He turned and pointed up to the screaming fans in the stands.

I looked up to see my mom hugging her husband, Greg. Grandpa was beaming as he wrapped his arm around Grandma. Brett was smiling—high fiving, Brittney. And Chad and Wes were giving me two thumbs up.

"It's obvious you're a fan favorite as well," the reporter continued loudly. "If you could pick one major thing you feel you owe your success to, what would that thing be?"

I didn't hesitate in my reply. "Chasing Nikki."

***

Don't miss the rest of Chase's story! Read the sequel, ***Finding Chase***, available December of 2012.

Author's Note:

Nikki's tragic death from pulmonary embolism is a very real occurrence after injuries. Sadly, many injuries that are not life threatening can end in this terrible result if not treated properly.

I experienced this heartbreak in my own life, after my mother fell from a ladder and broke her back. She was in a lot of pain which made it difficult for her move. She spent several weeks in physical therapy, trying to overcome her injury, but had a second bad spell. Due to her lack of efficient movement, she developed a blood clot and passed her first pulmonary embolism. She was placed in the hospital and treated for her condition, but, unfortunately, the damage was done. She died a week later of second massive pulmonary embolism—the day after she was released.

Hospitals routinely try to treat for this condition after accidents, which have helped lower the occurrence of this significantly. However, incorrect dosages and/or extenuating circumstances can still allow this killer to strike unexpectedly.

For more information on pulmonary embolism, its causes, signs. symptoms, and appropriate prevention, you can visit the Mayo Clinic's Website at:

http://www.mayoclinic.com/health/pulmonary-embolism/DS00429/DSECTION=prevention

If you have recently experienced the loss of loved one, there are many grief/counseling services available to help. You can search the internet to find a group or service near you.

About the Author

Lacey Weatherford is the bestselling author of the popular young adult paranormal romance series, Of Witches and Warlocks and Crush. She has always loved books and wanted to become a writer ever since reading her first Nancy Drew novel at the age of eight.

Lacey resides in the beautiful White Mountains of Arizona. She lives with her wonderful husband and children. When she's not out supporting one of her kids at their sporting/music events, she spends her time reading, writing, blogging, and socializing with her readers on her social media accounts.

Visit Lacey's Official Website for Apps, Books, News, and more:
http://www.laceyweatherfordbooks.com
Follow on Twitter:
LMWeatherford
Or Facebook:
Lacey Jackson Weatherford

Other books by Lacey Weatherford:

The Of Witches and Warlocks series
*The Trouble with Spells, The Demon Kiss,
Blood of the White Witch, The Dark Rising,
Possession of Souls*

Chasing Nikki, Finding Chase

Crush

*A Midsummer Night's
Fling*

Printed in Great Britain
by Amazon.co.uk, Ltd.,
Marston Gate.